MW00324816

THE LOVE OF HIS BROTHER

THE LOVE OF HIS BROTHER

JENNIFER ALLEE

FIVE STAR

An imprint of Thomson Gale, a part of The Thomson Corporation

THOMSON

GALE

Detroit • New York • San Francisco • New Haven, Conn. • Waterville, Maine • London

LONGWOOD PUBLIC LIBRARY

Copyright © 2007 by Jennifer L. AlLee.

Thomson Gale is part of The Thomson Corporation.

Thomson and Star Logo and Five Star are trademarks and Gale is a registered trademark used herein under license.

ALL RIGHTS RESERVED

This novel is a work of fiction. Names, characters, places and incidents are either the product of the author's imagination, or, if real, used fictitiously.

No part of this book may be reproduced or transmitted in any form or by any electronic or mechanical means, including photocopying, recording or by any information storage and retrieval system, without the express written permission of the publisher, except where permitted by law.

Set in 11 pt. Plantin.

LIBRARY OF CONGRESS CATALOGING-IN-PUBLICATION DATA

AlLee, Jennifer.
  The love of his brother / Jennifer AlLee. — 1st ed.
    p. cm.
  ISBN-13: 978-1-59414-609-1 (hardcover : alk. paper)
  ISBN-10: 1-59414-609-8 (hardcover : alk. paper)
  1. Widows—Family. I. Title.
PS3601.I39L68 2007
813'.6—dc22   2007022628

First Edition. First Printing: November 2007.

Published in 2007 in conjunction with Tekno Books.

Printed in the United States of America on permanent paper
10 9 8 7 6 5 4 3 2 1

To my husband, Marcus.
Without your love and support, there would be no book.

Prologue

The bell signaling the end of fourth-period algebra cut through the classroom, and twenty teenage bodies sprang to their feet almost simultaneously as they escaped their last class before lunch. One bright-eyed girl led the pack, having more serious matters than food on her mind.

The quad had filled up quickly with students pouring out of other rooms, but Whitney had no trouble finding the person she was looking for. She had developed a kind of radar where he was concerned. It seemed every time she looked around the campus her eyes zeroed in on him even if she wasn't trying to seek him out, so why should today be any different?

He was at the water fountain, folding his tall frame down to get a quick drink. As he lifted his head, a few drops of water fell from his lips and he swiped the back of his hand absently across his mouth as he headed toward his locker. There was going to be a pep rally that day, so he wore his football jersey, number 56. How many times had she written that number on her book covers and notebooks, only to hurriedly scratch it out in the fear that someone might notice? If anyone told him how she felt, she'd just die.

Whitney shook her head. If she stood there staring at him any longer, she wouldn't have to worry about it . . . she was making it pretty obvious that she was madly in love with the school's top quarterback.

She took a deep breath and commanded her feet to move.

She'd waited as long as she could, but that blasted dance was only two days away, and if she didn't ask now it would be too late. Whoever came up with the bright idea of making it "girl's choice" should have his head examined.

In a moment, Whitney was at her locker, which, by some divine miracle, was only one down and three over from his. As she knelt down to open it, she threw out the most casual greeting she could manage.

"Hi, Doug."

He turned and grinned at her. "Hey, Whit. How's it going?"

Her heart leapt just to hear him say her name. She dumped her books in the locker, slammed it shut and jumped to her feet. "Great," she answered, hoping the smile on her face didn't look quite as big as it felt. "I'm just looking forward to the weekend. Are you all set for the game?"

"Yep. I'm ready to kick some Wildcat butt," he answered, referring to the rival team. Then he turned toward her, leaning his shoulder against his closed locker door. "Are you going to be cheering us on?"

It's now or never, she told herself. "You bet I will. By the way," she said, trying to sound nonchalant, "are you going to the dance Saturday night?"

He pushed off the locker and made a face. "Yeah. I wasn't going to at first, but Shawna asked me. So I figured, why not?"

If she had ever felt worse in her life, Whitney couldn't remember when. But she kept that stupid smile plastered on her face and forced her voice to remain steady. "Yeah, well, great. Then I'll see you there."

"Cool. Hey, I gotta go. See ya later, kiddo." He flashed another grin and he was gone.

Whitney watched him walk toward the parking lot. Obviously, he was going to exercise his senior privilege and go off campus for lunch. And if she didn't feel bad enough already, things got even worse when she saw Shawna bound up to him. She was ready for the pep rally too, wearing her tight cheerleader sweater and short pleated skirt. Her mane of lustrous blond hair swirled around her shoulders as she jumped into Doug's arms. Whitney heard him growl playfully as he swung Shawna around, and then the two walked off to his car, their arms entwined.

Kiddo. He'd called her kiddo. Whitney could feel the heat building behind her eyes. He wouldn't have gone with her anyway, even if he didn't already have a date. After all, with a choice between the beautiful head cheerleader and a gangly freshman, it was obvious what his choice would be. It didn't help that he and Whitney had grown up together and they were almost like brother and sister. But that had all changed for Whitney on the first magical day when she'd walked onto the high school campus. She'd been standing with a group of freshman girls, all new and nervous, when Doug walked by. He'd smiled just at her and said, "Welcome to the big time, Whit," and kept right on walking. She'd never forget the looks on her friends' faces at the fact that popular, gorgeous Doug Poulten had singled her out. She'd fallen in love with him on the spot, and any sisterly feelings she'd ever had for him were forgotten.

But now it was painfully obvious to Whitney that his feelings hadn't changed. He'd always been like a protective big brother to her, and now was no different.

Well, at least I made the effort, she thought with a sigh. But then she realized that her problems were far from over. She'd told him she'd see him at the dance. Now she had two days to produce a date, or go stag and be mortified.

"Just great," she muttered, turning to stalk off toward the cafeteria. Instead she ran into a solid mass that grunted out a greeting as she hit it.

"Whitney, I've been looking for you."

She looked up into the face of Cliff Poulten, Doug's younger brother. They stood there with the wind knocked out of each other, and at that moment Whitney realized that even though she'd grown up with Cliff too, he wasn't looking at her like a big brother.

The smile that just a few moments before had been reserved only for Doug, slowly spread across her face.

"Hi, Cliff."

CHAPTER 1

The flower was little more than a shapeless lavender blur as Whitney peered through the viewfinder of her camera. She adjusted the focus until the image became sharp and crisp. Now the lady's slipper looked like the perfect thing to encase a fairy's dainty foot. A fat black bee chose that moment to buzz lazily into the frame, and Whitney smiled to herself as she gently pressed the shutter release. This one would definitely come in handy later. If only Cliff . . .

She rose quickly from her crouched position, scaring away the bee and straining a muscle in her thigh at the same time. She'd told herself she wouldn't do this anymore. This constant wishing and wondering didn't help anything. All it did was waste her energy and leave her feeling worse than she had before.

Yet Whitney couldn't help but think of what this day would be like if Cliff was still alive. He'd always gone with her on her picture-hunting excursions. In fact, often while Whitney was on the prowl for the perfect shot, Cliff would get the creative brainstorm he needed to start writing his next book. She had always found it interesting that instead of the story inspiring the illustrations, it was usually the other way around with them. She couldn't count the number of times they'd curled up on the couch together to look over her photographs and sketches until finally one would catch Cliff's eye, and he would begin to spin tales. "What if this butterfly was really a princess in disguise?" he'd say, or, "What if this fox has a wife and three cubs to support? That would account for his lean and hungry look."

"What if" was always one of Cliff's favorite lines. Whitney sighed at the thought of it. You couldn't spend every day of your married life with someone and not pick up some of his habits.

So, even though she knew better, Whitney indulged herself, just for a moment, and let her mind wander. What if, she thought, it was all really a terrible mistake? What if the plane hadn't really gone down? What if the pilot made an emergency landing and it's taken Cliff all this time just to get back to me? What if I walk into the house and there he is, standing in front of the window like he always used to do? In her mind, Whitney lived out the whole reunion. She could see herself rushing into his arms and melting in his embrace. She would touch his arms and his face, just to make sure he was real. And then his lips, the lips that had greeted her so many times before, that she knew so well, would burn against hers. . . .

"Cliff."

The sound of her voice startled her. She had been so far gone in her own fantasy that she had lost track of where she was and the reality of her situation. Now it all came flooding back—the pain twice as intense as before, reminding Whitney why she had promised herself never to indulge in answering the question "What if?"

She shook her head sharply. "That's enough of that," she commanded herself. "Get back to work, Poulten."

She started off up the trail, but was alerted by the sound of something crashing through the trees. She whirled around, not so much from fear as a desire to be in position to take a picture of whatever was going to run out of the foliage. A moment later, she dropped her camera to her side, shaking her head and trying not to laugh.

"What are you doing so far from home, Digger?"

In answer Digger, so named because of all the plants and

flowers he'd dug up as a puppy, wagged his tail furiously. Whitney knew what was coming, but she was too late to stop it.

"Digger, down!"

The words were barely out of her mouth when the big dog barked three times, gathered himself together, and hurled himself at Whitney. Digger planted his muddy paws firmly on the front of her white T-shirt and licked her face enthusiastically. It took a bit of effort, but Whitney finally succeeded in getting the huge mutt off her.

"Good dog," she said when he was sitting calmly. Then she glanced down at the front of her shirt. "Ugh." She glared at Digger, ready to scold him, but couldn't. With his head cocked to the side and his tongue lolling out of the corner of his mouth, he looked like he was laughing at a very funny joke. So instead of telling him what she thought of the mess he'd made, she scratched him behind the ear.

"If you weren't just a dumb animal, I'd have your hide. Then again, you're probably a lot smarter than I am. You wouldn't wear white into a wet, muddy forest, would you?"

Digger barked and licked her arm in response. She laughed. "I didn't think so. Come on!" She slapped her thigh, signaling the big dog to follow her. "Let's take you home, and then I can clean up a bit too."

Digger was her in-laws' dog, and Whitney knew she probably would have ended up at their house even if she hadn't had her run-in with the pooch. Just the thought of Hank and Myra Poulten made Whitney smile. They'd been like her second parents during her growing up years and had filled the gap when at age fifteen her father decided to leave his wife and daughter in search of himself. When they found out that Cliff and Whitney were engaged, it was almost difficult to tell which couple was more excited. Before the wedding, Whitney and Cliff had spent many an evening with them, sitting around the

kitchen table or sprawled in the living room going over prepara-
tions for the ceremony. One evening, when Myra asked them
where they planned to live, Whitney and Cliff had exchanged
blank glances, hoping the other would have the answer, but
neither of them did.

"This is going to sound silly," Cliff said sheepishly, "but we
haven't really talked about it."

The grins that broke out on his parents' faces then had been
nothing short of comical. When Hank looked like he was ready
to burst, he shot out, "Well, we were going to try to keep this a
surprise for a little longer, but it looks like the cat's clawing its
way out of the bag! Cliff, Whitney, . . . Mother and I have
decided that our wedding gift to you is going to be three acres
at the edge of our property."

Not only had they given them the land, but all the relatives
had gotten together and figured out that what newlyweds really
needed wasn't crystal bowls or silver bud vases; what they really
needed was a home. So Uncle Harry, the contractor, worked
with Cousin Sherman, who ran the mill, and they built the nic-
est two-bedroom home any young couple could want. Grandma
Emma, who was still the sharpest accountant in all of Lincoln
County, and quite possibly the entire state of Montana, kept
track of the money given toward the project by the remaining
members of the extensive Poulten family clan.

Even then, the couple had still ended up with three electric
can openers, two crystal salad bowls, a silver electroplate cake
tray, and a kitchen clock shaped like a rooster.

It didn't take long for Whitney and Digger to get to the main
house of the Poulten ranch. The dog looked up at her as if to
ask, "Can I go now?" She smiled and scratched the top of his
head. "Okay, go on. But try to stay around home. And keep
your dirty paws off people."

As she went up the front steps of the house, she was vaguely aware that the long driveway was more crowded than usual. The old station wagon closest to the house belonged to Jeannie Poulten. If she was there, then her twin Sarah was probably with her. The two lived just down the road in a duplex, the irony of which they loved pointing out to people. It wasn't uncommon for Whitney to find the sisters at their parents' home, especially in the morning. But the brand-new pickup truck parked behind the station wagon didn't belong there. Someone must have come up from town. As she wiped her muddy feet on the welcome mat, her thoughts seemed to be confirmed by the commotion going on inside. And since her in-laws' house was like her second home, she didn't think twice about letting herself in.

The front door opened into a small service area where you could leave dirty boots and shoes during the wet months. In a corner she saw two suitcases and a leather briefcase. Whoever was here must be staying for a visit. She walked farther into the house and discovered that the jumble of voices came from the Poulten family standing in a tight circle, surrounding someone in the middle of the living room. And from the way they were gesturing as they talked, they seemed to be pretty worked up about something.

"Hey," Whitney called, making her presence known. "What's all the excitement about?"

At the sound of her voice everyone stopped talking and turned around. The move made her think of the parting of the Red Sea. And there in the middle of them stood the cause of the commotion. Whitney gasped.

"Doug."

It had been years since Whitney had seen her brother-in-law, but it appeared that little had changed. He still had a confident air about him and a slightly crooked grin. He came forward, all smiles, and gave her a big hug. "I seem to be shocking everybody today. It's good to see you, Whitney."

"Hello, Doug," she said flatly. As he stepped back from her, she got some perverse satisfaction out of the fact that there was now dirt all over the front of his white shirt.

"Sorry," she muttered, sounding anything but.

He looked down and shrugged. "Oh well, like Cliff always said, 'Never trust a man with a clean shirt.' He may not have been much of an athlete, but he always could come up with a good line. I guess that's why he turned out to be the writer of the family. By the way, how's your painting going?"

Whitney knew her jaw was clenched and she was staring at him, but she felt as if she'd just been slapped. How could he be so cavalier, talking about Cliff as if he were just in the other room instead of gone from the earth? She was afraid if she stayed there with him another second, she was going to be sick.

"I've got to go," she stammered as she backed toward the door.

Myra Poulten held a hand out to her. "Whitney, dear, please wait—"

Whitney shook her head. "I can't. I . . . uh . . . bye."

She ran out the door, not bothering to pull it closed, and pushed through the screen door. It swung shut and slammed with a bang as she ran down the steps, into the trees, and back down the trail to her house.

Doug ran one hand down his face. He was too tired to make heads or tails out of what was going on with his family. All he really wanted to do was find an empty bed and sleep in it for many uninterrupted hours.

He knew it was his own fault. He should have called his parents and told them he was on his way. But he hadn't wanted the first time they spoke in years to be over the phone. As soon as he'd gotten his affairs in order, he'd bought a new pickup, packed it with his few worldly possessions, and hit the road. He'd wasted enough time over the past few years. The last thing he wanted to do was waste any more by planning.

It had been a long time since Doug Poulten had been home, but for the most part the place was just as he'd remembered it. His family, always boisterous, didn't disappoint him. As soon as he'd walked through the door, they'd surrounded him, all talking at once. They'd bombarded him with questions, but hadn't given him a chance to answer many of them. Then, in the middle of it all, Whitney had come in. Now, *she* had changed. Always quick with a hug and a smile, he'd expected a much different welcome from her. He couldn't figure out why she was so cold to him. And where in the heck was Cliff?

"What's with her?" Doug turned to his parents, bemused. "I've never seen her act that way before."

"Oh, Doug," his mother answered. "How could you have done that?"

Doug noticed she was twisting the corner of her apron in her hands. Everybody was certainly overreacting to a friendly conversation. "Done what?" he asked innocently.

His sister Sarah stood with her arms crossed, glaring at him. "That was pretty cold, Doug."

He turned in confusion to his father. "Dad, is this a female thing that I'm not getting? What did I do?"

Hank Poulten's face was set like stone. "That was a very callous thing you did, talking about your brother that way."

Doug's eyes lifted toward the ceiling. "That? That's what's bothering everybody? Cliff and I always talk to each other like that. Besides, I was complimenting him."

"That may be," Hank said, "but consider Whitney's feelings. And ours too, for that matter. None of us have had one word from you since the accident, and to hear you say what you just did—"

"Wait a minute," Doug interrupted. "What accident?"

The silence that filled the room snaked around them like a living thing. Jeannie opened her mouth to speak, but when no words came out she snapped it shut and stuffed her hands in the back pockets of her jeans. Sarah stared at Doug as if he had just announced that he was from another planet, and in fact that was almost how he felt. His parents, meanwhile, stood looking helplessly at each other. As Doug studied them, he now saw that they had changed, after all. His father was grayer than he'd remembered, and he wasn't standing as ramrod straight as he used to. His mother, who had almost always had a smile on her face, now had a hint of sadness in her eyes. What had happened while he'd been gone?

Finally, Hank found his voice. "You mean you don't know?"

"No." Doug's voice was strong and steady, much steadier than he felt. He had no idea what this accident they were talking about was, but if it had anything to do with his brother, he wasn't so sure he wanted to find out.

"I'm sorry, son." Doug could see that Myra was trying not to cry. "I wish you didn't have to find out this way. We were just so sure you knew. I mean, we sent you so many letters. When we didn't hear from you, we just assumed you were . . . too busy."

"I haven't had a letter from you in months. In fact, I hardly ever got any mail. It was hard to catch up with me, I guess. I traveled around with the stable so much, going from track to track, I—" Doug cut himself off. He knew he was rambling, trying to put off hearing what they had to say. He wanted to tell them, "If I can't do anything to change it, then I don't want to know." But instead he looked his mother in the eye and said, "Mom, where is Cliff? What happened to him?"

"He . . ." she began, but broke off, unable to go on.

Doug then looked to his father. "Dad?"

Hank took a deep breath. "Cliff was in an accident, about

two months ago. He was in a small plane on the last leg of a trip back from New York and . . . son, the plane went down. Cliff didn't make it."

Doug heard his father's words, but part of his mind refused to believe them. "Didn't make it?"

Sarah, practical as always, saw his need to cut through the euphemisms. Gently she told him, "Cliff is dead."

No, Doug's mind insisted. Cliff couldn't be dead. Cliff was solid and steady and always around when Doug needed him. There were so many things he'd wanted to talk to Cliff about now that he was back home. Things he'd learned about himself. Some things he needed to apologize for. But how could he do that now? No, Cliff couldn't be dead. But he looked at his family, and the grief in their eyes told him it was true. Now he understood why Whitney had acted the way she did.

"Whitney!" He snapped out of it, remembering her, the pained, almost scared look on her face. How he must have hurt her. "I've got to go talk to her."

He started for the door, but his father gently grabbed his arm. "Why don't you let her be for a while? Give her some time to herself, and give yourself time to deal with this."

Doug pulled away from his father's grasp, shaking his head sharply. How could he explain the inadequacy he felt? They'd just told him his brother was dead, and there was nothing he could do to change it. He was helpless. But Whitney was alive and he had hurt her. Here was something concrete that he could focus on. This was something he could fix. "Until I make things right with Whitney, I won't be able to even think about my feelings for Cliff, much less deal with them."

"But son, there's something you need to know!" Hank called after him, but Doug heard only half of it. Whatever it was, it could wait. Doug was already out the door and running down the same path Whitney had taken just a few minutes earlier.

CHAPTER 2

Whitney seethed as she walked back toward home. Her camera, hanging by its strap from her shoulder, beat out a hollow rhythm against her hip, but she barely noticed it. She was too busy ranting at the mental image of Doug Poulten.

"Of all the no good, inconsiderate things to say. I've known you were a self-centered louse ever since you took off without a word of good-bye to anybody. And for what? To train a bunch of horses so they could chase each other's tails around a track! I should have known you wouldn't change."

Her steps slowed as her last statement sunk in. Why had she expected anything different from him? A long time ago, he had been a kind, considerate kid. But somewhere in his adolescence he had changed. She guessed that becoming one of the most noticeable athletes in their high school had managed to inflate his ego to an all-time high, because ever since then, he'd been different. He was concerned only about himself—about his image, his future—and he did something only if he knew that Douglas T. Poulten would benefit from it.

More than once Doug had told her and Cliff how he was planning to go to college on a football scholarship and from there play pro ball. But an injury during the middle of the season in his senior year had burst that dream. Never much interested in academics, he'd given up the idea of going to college and instead focused on working with horses, the only other thing that truly excited him. He had turned out to be a gifted trainer and quickly worked his way up through the local racetracks and fairs.

It was no surprise to anybody that he would want to move on to bigger tracks where the stakes were higher. What did surprise everybody was how he went away. Not a word to anybody, just a note left for his parents. Whitney still remembered consoling Myra the day they realized he'd gone.

"It's not that a mother expects her kids to stay around forever," Myra had said, wiping the tears from her eyes. "But a proper good-bye would have been nice."

He'd been away for eight years, and in all that time had sent only two letters to his parents. He'd proven just how little he cared about anybody but himself.

So why should now be any different?

"Because Cliff was your brother," she muttered under her breath.

She hadn't gone much farther when she heard leaves being crushed under foot. From the sound of it, the feet were behind her and were coming at a pretty good clip. Out of reflex she put her hand to her camera and turned around. What she saw made her wish briefly that she were fingering a gun in a holster rather than a camera hanging from a strap.

"Go away!" she yelled at Doug, who was running at breakneck speed through the undergrowth. She quickened her pace, hoping he would get the message.

But instead of giving up, he just came after her faster.

"Whitney, wait! I've got to talk to you!"

No way, buster, her mind screamed. Whitney refused to waste any more breath on him. Besides, she needed all she had, because now she was running from him as quickly as she could. She was sure to have black and blue marks from the camera slapping against her hip, but she didn't care. She just wanted Doug to leave her alone.

She looked over her shoulder, hoping she wouldn't see him anymore. He was there, but she was surprised when he pulled himself to a dead stop, waved his arms in the air, and yelled, "Whitney, look out!"

By the time she looked back at where she was going, it was already too late to miss the hollow in the path that had been turned into a mud hole by the last rain. Her tennis shoe sank into it, she felt her ankle twist, her center of gravity shifted, and down she went.

Doug ran up to her, stopping just short of the mud. "Hey, are you all right?"

She rolled over slowly, making no move to check her camera, which was buried deep in the mud. Instead her hand went to her abdomen, beginning at the left and moving in a slow trajectory all the way across to the right. Her formerly white cotton shirt was wet with mud and plastered to her skin, emphasizing the small bulge beneath it. She heard Doug suck in a deep, shocked breath. He was staring at her, and when he finally spoke, his eyes never left her stomach.

"Whitney, you're . . . are you . . . ?"

"Yes," she said sharply, "I'm pregnant."

He went down on his knees, reaching out to help her up. He didn't seem to care that his pants were now soaked from the knees down. "Are you okay? Do you think the baby—"

"I'm fine and the baby is fine. As if you really cared."

"Come on, Whitney. If I thought I caused anything to happen to you or your baby, I couldn't live with myself."

"Why you—" she cut herself off long enough to throw a well-aimed handful of mud at him, hitting his cheek. "You didn't care enough about your own brother to even attend his funeral! Why would you worry if anything happened to me? Are you afraid I'd try to sue you? Well don't worry. I wouldn't waste my time."

"Listen," he continued, wiping the mud away with the back of his shirtsleeve, "that's why I followed you. I wanted to explain what happened back at the house."

She could see how frustrated he was, but that was the least of her concerns. "Oh," she said, her voice dripping with sarcasm, "you wanted to let me know that the only reason you said those things was because you're an unthinking, self-centered jerk? You didn't need to bother. I figured that out already."

He shifted one leg, raising a knee out of the wet dirt. "You know, I'd much rather have this talk in a warm room, wearing clean clothes, maybe even sharing a cup of coffee. But this is where we are, and I don't think we should go anywhere else until we work this out."

Whitney looked away from him. She didn't care about his opinion or the fact that he was uncomfortable. Then she caught sight of her camera. "This is just great," she muttered, pulling it out of the mud with a sucking sound.

Despite the fact that she ignored him, he pressed on. "You don't understand, Whitney. I'd hardly been home for more than ten minutes when you walked in. My folks barely had time to say hello to me, much less . . ."

He stopped talking, and Whitney knew he wanted her to acknowledge him, to at least look at him, but she couldn't. She was too upset to trust herself with what she might say. So she just examined her camera, despite the fact that she didn't know what she was looking for.

"Whitney, listen to me!" He fairly shouted in her face as he yanked the camera out of her hands and tossed it aside.

There was no ignoring him now. She whipped her head around to face him, but before she could open her mouth, Doug continued.

"What happened back at the house was a mistake. I didn't know anything about Cliff's accident until today."

Her lips felt tight and she stared at him blankly, taking in this new information. "How could you not have known?" she asked stiffly. "I wrote to you. So did Mom and Dad. And Sarah, and—"

"I know. Believe it or not, I never got any of those letters. I was moving around too much." Doug ran a hand through his hair, finding a mud clot in the process. "I know I've done a lot of stupid, selfish things in my life, but I'm not a monster. If I'd known what happened to Cliff, I would have been home in a heartbeat."

They stayed that way for a while, neither of them moving, their eyes locked. Finally, Whitney's lashes dipped and she looked away from Doug, breaking the standoff.

"How about it, Whit? Do you accept my apology?"

She looked at him, obviously surprised by his use of her old nickname. He hadn't called her Whit since they were kids. "You don't need to apologize," she said. "It seems that I've just made a colossal fool out of myself. I'm sorry I jumped to conclusions without giving you a chance to explain. That's one thing about being pregnant. It tends to make you highly emotional."

Doug grinned. "I'm not so sure pregnancy has anything to do with it. My father jumped to the same conclusions, and I know he's not expecting."

They laughed together at the ridiculous image of Hank Poulten great with child. And then, when the humor wore off, Whitney realized she had more than one reason to be embarrassed. She was sure she must look like an old sow wallowing in the muck.

"Well," she said, attempting to feign brightness, "I think I've had about all the mud I can take for one day. How 'bout you?"

"Agreed." Doug rose smoothly and held out his hand. "Here, let me help you up."

"That's all right, I'm fine." No matter how ridiculous she looked, Whitney was determined to stand up by herself. And she did just that, until she put some weight on her left foot. The pain that shot through her made her jerk backward, throwing her off balance again.

At the sight of her teetering, Doug jumped forward, deeper into the mud, and kept her from going over. "So, you're okay, huh?" He couldn't keep a tinge of smugness out of his voice.

Whitney pulled her shoulder away from him. "Yes, I am. I just twisted my ankle a little, that's all."

As if to prove that nothing was wrong, she took a step forward and found out how incredibly hard it is to smile and grit your teeth at the same time.

Before she knew it, Doug had scooped her up in his arms and they were trudging out of the slop.

"What do you think you're doing?" she asked hotly.

"I think I'm carrying you back to your home before you do even more damage to your ankle."

"But I told you—"

"Can it, Whitney. What you told me was a lie." She glared at him, and he couldn't help but chuckle. "Okay, maybe 'lie' is too strong a word. How 'bout this. What you told me was a falsehood. I saw the look on your face when you put some weight on that ankle. Underneath all that mud you went whiter than Glacier Park in winter."

Well, she thought, he's got me on that one. "But I'm too heavy to lug through the forest." That was a lame excuse, she knew. Especially since he was carrying her like she weighed nothing at all. She was going to have to think of something better than that. "Besides . . . I'm filthy!"

"Will you hush? Even pregnant you weigh hardly anything. And as far as filthy goes, I couldn't get much dirtier than I already am. So just relax and enjoy the ride, all right?"

She waited a moment before conceding. "Oh, all right."

She kept her mouth shut during the rest of the trip to her

house. Whitney would never admit it, but she was just a little bit glad that he hadn't let her try to walk it out. Her ankle throbbed even without putting any pressure on it.

It didn't take long to reach Whitney's home. The rustic looking cabin, flanked by a more modern-style garage, seemed to appear out of nowhere in the middle of the woods. Doug walked up to the door and shifted Whitney's weight in his arms. "Can you reach your key?"

"I don't need to." She reached down, turned the knob, and swung the door open.

He frowned, shaking his head, but didn't say a word. Instead he carried her through the living room and straight down the hallway to the bathroom. Once inside, he set her gently on the side of the tub.

"Do you have an elastic bandage?"

She had to think for a moment, not sure if she'd ever used one before. "I think there's one in the linen closet, in the hall."

Doug left the bathroom. A moment later she could hear him rummaging around in her things. When he came back, there was a triumphant look on his face and a rolled bandage in his hand. He set it on the sink.

"There you go. What you need to do is get washed up, wrap your ankle and relax. I think you've had a pretty trying day." His smile was warm, and concern was apparent in his eyes.

Whitney looked at him in amazement. This was not the same Doug Poulten who had taken off without thinking of anybody else all those years ago. And she felt like a heel. She had treated him so badly, yet he was still trying to make sure that she was okay. Now, as he turned to leave, something in her couldn't let him go. Not like this.

"Doug."

He stopped. "Yes."

"Would you mind waiting till I get out of here? I really think we need to talk."

She could tell her request surprised him, but he simply nodded and left the room.

He left the bathroom, closing the door behind him. In a second, he could hear the water running. Doug looked down at the mud caked on his shirt.

"I need to be hosed off," he muttered.

Since there was only one bathroom in the house, Doug did what he considered to be sensible. He peeled off his shirt, leaving it to soak in the kitchen sink, and washed himself the best he could with a clean dishrag. Then, since the house felt like the next best thing to a refrigerator, he decided to start a fire.

As he waited for Whitney to finish, Doug wandered around the living room. The place was still as homey as he'd remembered it. He'd been there the day before he'd left for California. He could still recall how flushed Whitney had looked when she'd answered the door, as if he had interrupted something. And then a moment later Cliff had come out of the bedroom to join them. Doug didn't remember what they'd talked about that day, except for the fact that he hadn't told them he was leaving. It was the last time he had seen Cliff.

Now Doug moved restlessly around the room, seeing things that had belonged to his kid brother and slowly coming to the realization that he would never see him again. Hung in a prominent spot over the mantle was an award that Cliff had won for one of his children's books. Sadly, Doug realized he had never taken an interest in Cliff's work. Never had he read any of the books that Cliff and Whitney collaborated on. Once, when they were teenagers, Cliff had tried to tell Doug how he felt when he wrote. He had tried to explain to Doug the exhilaration of creating people and places and things out of nothing more than a wisp of an idea, and seeing them take

27

shape and become something. But instead of making an effort to understand his brother, to share in what he loved, Doug had brushed Cliff's revelations off.

"Yeah, well, I'll take sports any day. And we'll see what the girls like more—your brain or my muscles!"

Doug shuddered as he remembered the coldness of his comeback. At the time, he couldn't imagine anything being more of a rush than football was to him, so he didn't even try. But now more than anything he wished he could talk to Cliff and tell him how sorry he was for the way he'd treated him. It was one of the reasons he'd come back in the first place. To make amends. But he was too late. Doug crouched down in front of the fire, staring into the flames, losing himself in thought.

I'm so sorry, Cliff. I never meant to hurt you the way I did, but Whitney's right. I was self-centered and I didn't think about anybody but myself. I just wish I could let you know how much I really love you.

"I love you, brother."

It came out of him in a rasping whisper, and with it came the relief of tears, the tangible expression of the sorrow that was filling him.

Behind him he heard a cough. Doug turned to see Whitney standing in the hall behind him. Her hair hung limply around her face in damp strands, and she was almost swallowed up by a dark blue terry cloth robe. It was so big, he was sure it had been Cliff's.

She gave him a weak smile, as if she was embarrassed for walking in on him. "I'm all cleaned up."

Doug jumped up and was at her side in a flash. "Well for Pete's sake, woman, sit down!"

He led her over to the couch and sat beside her. "I hope you don't mind me starting the fire. I rinsed my shirt out in your sink, but then I realized it was colder than a well digger's . . . well, you know." You're rambling again, he thought. Better just to shut up.

But Whitney smiled at him. "The fire's nice. If you hadn't started it, I would have. Thanks."

An uncomfortable silence fell in the room. They were both stiff, both waiting for the other to say something. Finally Whitney blurted out, "Well, I bet you're wondering why I wanted to talk to you."

"It had crossed my mind."

She'd been picking at the lint on her robe, but now she stopped and looked him in the eye. "I just wanted you to know how sorry I am for treating you so badly. And I wanted to make sure that you're okay."

"Okay?"

"Yes. About Cliff, I mean." He looked away, but she kept on. "I know it was a tremendous shock, and you found out about it in the worst way. I just want you to know that if you need to talk . . . well, you can talk to me."

Doug looked back at her, his heart full of affection for his sister-in-law. She had gone through so much already, yet here she was, thinking of him. But he wasn't about to burden her now with his problems. "I'll be fine, really. To tell you the truth, I'm more concerned about you." He glanced down at her stomach. "When did you find out you were pregnant?"

She hesitated, then answered, "About two weeks after Cliff's funeral."

His heart broke a little more, for his brother never knowing of his child, and for Whitney, never being able to share even a moment of the joy with her husband. "That must have been terrible for you."

"It was . . . but then it wasn't." She looked away from Doug, staring across the room as though she could see Cliff there.

"Cliff and I wanted children so much. We'd been trying to conceive for about a year and a half. And then, to find out after he was gone that the thing we'd been praying for was going to happen . . . I was so angry at first. At myself for not getting pregnant sooner. At Cliff for not being here when I need him. At God for taking him from me."

She turned back to Doug, and in the midst of her pain, a radiance showed on her face. "But then I realized that what happened was an awful accident. It wasn't Cliff's fault, or mine, or God's. And I realized how blessed I am. I'm carrying the gift of life, and a part of Cliff that will live on, even though he's gone."

Doug shook his head. "I don't know how you do it."

She forced a smile. "Easy. It's either see the good where I can find it or curl up in a corner and die. And believe me, I've considered that too."

They were quiet, and once again Doug felt uncomfortable. He'd been away for such a long time, and there were so many things to say. But all of them paled in comparison to Whitney's honest admission of her feelings. Rather than continue down that road, he tried to pick a safe topic. "How's your ankle?"

She frowned. "To be honest, not so good. It's still throbbing."

"Let me take a look at it."

She winced as she put her foot on the coffee table. Doug took one look at it and burst out laughing.

Whitney looked offended. "What's so funny?"

"I have never seen anything as pitiful as that." He pointed at her ankle and the bandage that was loosely wrapped around it. In fact, it was so loose, the bandage actually hung off in spots. "That's going to do you as much good as if we'd left the bandage in the closet."

"I didn't want to wrap it too tight and cut off the circulation," she answered defensively.

Doug tried to look serious, but a smile still played at the corners of his mouth. "You'll be happy to know you're in no danger."

Whitney crossed her arms over her chest and scowled at him. "I've never had to wrap my ankle before. It's not my fault if I don't know how to do it."

"You're absolutely right," he said, trying to choke down his amusement. "Here, give me your foot and let me help you."

She looked at him uncertainly, but put her foot in his lap anyway. He removed the bandage, rerolled it, and then wrapped her ankle from scratch. Her foot felt warm and smooth under his calloused fingers.

"There," he announced when he had finished. "How's that?"

She looked at her ankle with a critical eye. "I hate to admit it, but you did a much better job than I did."

"It comes from years of practice." At the questioning look in her eyes, he continued. "I've wrapped many a fetlock in my day."

"I don't know if I like being lumped into the same category as a bunch of horses."

Doug wagged a finger at her. "Ah, but not just any horses. The horses I work with are worth hundreds of thousands of dollars. So you see, you're being lumped with the equestrian elite."

He could tell she was trying to stay miffed at him, but it didn't take long for her to crack. In a moment, she was smiling at him and he smiled back. This time, when the silence fell in the room it was companionable and not at all awkward. Until they both realized simultaneously that Doug's hand was still cradling Whitney's foot in his lap.

"Uh, thanks again," Whitney said, motioning at her ankle as she quickly moved it.

31

Just as quickly, Doug jumped to his feet. "Well, I guess I'd better get going and let you get some rest."

He was headed for the door when Whitney called out to him.

"Doug, wait. You can't go out like that."

He looked down, feeling ridiculous. He'd forgotten he was shirtless.

"Just a second." Whitney hobbled down the hall and came back a moment later. "Here."

He took the sweatshirt she held out to him. Something else Cliff had left behind. But the shirt that had been a bit baggy on Cliff fit Doug like a second skin.

"Thanks," he said. "I wouldn't want to be picked up by the forest service for indecent exposure."

Doug went to the door, turning to her before he went out. "Get some rest, Whit. And don't forget to lock up."

Whitney watched as he pulled the door shut behind him. With a shake of her head she turned, went back to the couch, and let herself fall onto it with a sigh. Staring into the fire, she couldn't help but remember her shock at walking in on Doug and finding him in the middle of such an emotional moment.

As he'd crouched before the fireplace, the glow from the flames played across the tensed muscles in his arms and chest. Whitney didn't know why she'd remained silent and studied him, but as she had, she realized there really wasn't much of a resemblance between Cliff and his brother. Cliff had been lean, but his build was soft and not well defined. Doug was larger, but every bit of him was solid muscle. Cliff's face had had such delicate features, he could almost have been considered pretty. On the other hand, the lines of Doug's face were harsher. His square jaw and tanned skin gave him a rugged look, and from the bump on his nose, Whitney would guess it had been broken at least once.

But what surprised Whitney the most was that, as she stood watching him in the glow of the fire, she was sure she saw tears glistening as they ran down his cheeks. The Doug she used to know would rather walk barefoot over broken glass than let his emotions show. Something had certainly changed him.

It had been quite a day. Her emotions were still churning, crashing around inside her head and her heart. She looked down at the bandage wrapped snuggly around her ankle and smiled. If only Cliff were here. He'd be so happy that Doug was home.

CHAPTER 3

Whitney perched half on and half off a tall stool in her studio, staring at the nearly completed canvas in front of her. Clipped to the top of the easel was the photograph she was using as inspiration. With a critical eye she looked at one, then the other, trying to find what it was about the painting that wasn't right. Finally she came to the conclusion that she hadn't missed a thing.

On canvas, the creek glistened and flowed just as it did in the photograph. The same stately pines towered in the background, reaching to the sky, which was the same untouched, vibrant shade of blue that only people who live in the country ever get a chance to see. She'd conveyed the photograph perfectly, down to the smallest detail.

No, it wasn't something that she had missed. It was something that was missing, period. From both the photo as well as the painting.

It wasn't any great surprise. As usually happened when Whitney took one of her photographs and transferred it to canvas, she had come to the point where it was time for her to add some detail that would make the painting uniquely different. Sometimes it was as small as changing the pattern in the clouds. Or it could be as large as creating a herd of wild horses thundering to regions unknown. What did shock Whitney was the realization that, this time, she had no idea what belonged there.

She looked around the room, as if she might find her much-needed muse curled up in a corner. But the sunlight that poured through the huge bay window dominating the east wall illuminated only a cluttered artist's studio that needed to be tidied. Badly.

"No inspiration there," she muttered.

She looked down at her pallet. Maybe the painting just needed a little color. Right now, it was mostly comprised of rugged earth tones. She swirled her brush through dollops of blue, then red, then white, and came up with a lovely shade of lavender. She smiled, looked at the painting, and then froze.

"What am I going to do with this? I know," she said sarcastically, "I could put a basket of Easter eggs under one of the trees."

She snorted in disgust and dropped her brush in a jar of thinner on the worktable beside her. As if it wasn't bad enough her imagination had fled, now she was talking to herself.

I wouldn't have to if Cliff were here, she thought. If he were there, she'd pull him in to have a look at the painting. Not that he'd know any better than she did what belonged in it, but at least he'd make her forget how frustrated she was. He always knew how to distract her, to take her mind off the thing that gnawed at her and get her to focus elsewhere. If Cliff was there, they'd—

"Stop it!" She got up so fast that her stool fell over with a crash, nearly making her jump out of her skin. It was an overreaction, she knew. But she couldn't keep rehashing the same old emotions. The fact of the matter was that Cliff was gone. And no amount of wishing would bring him back.

Whitney resisted the urge to throw her pallet on the table. The studio was messy enough already without adding spatters of oil paints on the floor. As she cleaned up today's mess and put away as much of the old mess as she felt moved to, she made an attempt to calm her frazzled nerves.

35

"I'm just lonely, so if talking to myself helps, then I guess it's okay. I hardly ever go out, and it's not like people are beating down my door to see me, so—"

Whitney stopped moving the broom that she had been halfheartedly sweeping the floor with. She could have sworn she'd heard something. Something that sounded like a knock on her front door.

"I really am losing my mind," she muttered.

Then she heard it again, and she knew it hadn't been her imagination. As she walked down the hall, she tried to think of who it could be, but she didn't have a clue. All her friends and family knew she wasn't in the habit of locking her door. Anybody who knew her would just walk right in.

When she opened the door, she couldn't stop the smile that jumped to her face. Doug stood outside, scowling and wagging a finger in her face.

"I didn't hear you undo the lock," he chided her.

"That's because it wasn't done in the first place." He began to shake his head furiously, evoking a burst of laughter from Whitney. "Do you want to come in, or would you rather stand outside and scold me all day?"

He transformed into his normal self, smiling pleasantly at her. "Thank you. I'd love to come in." He walked past her into the living room. As Whitney shut the door behind him, she noticed that he kept his hands behind his back. What is he up to now, she wondered.

"So, what brings you to my corner of the woods?"

"I've got something for you. After the other day, and our run-in with the mud hole, well . . ." The sharp wit that had come to him so easily before had vanished, and now he was practically stammering. She could almost see him mentally prod himself to continue. "Here you go."

With a quick movement he thrust out the object he'd been

hiding behind his back since he'd walked through the door.

"My camera," Whitney gasped.

In all the excitement and confusion the day he'd come home, she'd almost forgotten they'd left her precious camera face down in the mud. The next day, she'd tromped out to the woods to look for it, but it was gone. She'd assumed some animal had decided it would make a nice plaything and had dragged it off. Never had she thought that Doug might have been the one behind its disappearance. But what he held out to her now didn't bare any resemblance to the thrashed piece of equipment she'd seen two days ago. She reached for it cautiously, as if any sudden movement might transform it back into its former, muddy state.

"This is my camera, isn't it?"

He chuckled. "Yeah. I ran into it when I went back to the house, so I took it into town and had it cleaned up."

He made it sound like he'd dropped by a camera shop on his way home. But the closest town was half an hour away, and Whitney knew darned good and well there was no one there who knew anything about cleaning a camera, particularly one in as much peril as hers had been. The town he was referring to was a two-hour drive. In one direction. And of course no shop would have done a job like that for free.

Whitney was touched by the gesture. "You didn't need to go to so much trouble."

He shook his head. "I wanted to. It was the least I could do."

"But it wasn't your fault," she demanded. "At least let me pay you for it."

He looked skyward and crossed his arms over his chest. "Look, missy, I don't intend to fight over whose fault it was that the camera got a mud bath." The humor had come back to him and his eyes twinkled. "Just be gracious enough to accept my kindness, and let's change the subject. Agreed?"

She considered it and decided she'd be getting the better part of the deal if she went along with him. "Agreed," she said with a nod. "Now what do you want to talk about?"

"Hmm . . . you could tell me what you were doing when I showed up uninvited on your doorstep, but," he said with a grin, "I'll bet I can guess."

"Oh, can you?"

"Yep."

He seemed awfully certain of himself. He couldn't possibly know exactly what she'd been doing. "Okay. If you're so all knowing, go ahead and tell me."

He scratched his chin, scrutinizing her at great length before he said confidently, "You were painting. And you were using a very pretty shade of lavender too."

As quickly as she felt her mouth drop open she snapped it shut. "Were you peeping through my window?"

"I guess I'm going to have to confess." He lowered his voice as if disclosing a great secret. "You're wearing part of your creation on your face."

Her hand automatically went to her cheek, but Doug shook his head. "You missed it." He reached up and touched the tip of her nose.

The contact caught her by surprise and she jerked her head back. "Thanks for not telling me sooner." Her voice was heavy with sarcasm and she could feel the flush rising to her cheeks. If she didn't do something quickly, she knew she'd end up even more embarrassed than she already was. "I'd better go wash up."

She stalked off to the bathroom and left Doug standing in the living room, his shoulders shaking with silent laughter.

As Whitney looked at herself in the mirror over the sink, she found it was worse than she'd thought. Oh, the paint on her face wasn't so bad. The lavender smudge on the tip of her nose was probably the result of relieving an itch at the wrong time. What was really bad was the way the rest of her looked. Morning sickness combined with the fact that she lived alone had made Whitney become very lax about her at-home appearance. After waking up late in the morning, she'd taken a quick shower and put her hair up in a ponytail while it was still wet. Now that it was dry, some of it had escaped the elastic band that held it and hung around her face in strawlike clumps. And the clothes she wore were no better. Her black sweat pants and red-checked flannel shirt were both shapeless and covered with old and new paint stains.

"You look like something the cat wouldn't even bother to drag in," she muttered to her reflection.

As she washed her face it crossed her mind that she shouldn't be so concerned about the way she looked. After all, Doug was family, and family would understand why she looked like a ragamuffin in the middle of the afternoon.

She patted her face dry and spotted the basket full of clean clothes on top of the hamper. She'd done them a couple of days ago, but still hadn't gotten around to putting them away. For once, procrastination had paid off.

Whitney stripped off her work clothes and threw them into a corner. Sure, family was supposed to look past clothing that probably should have been donated to the Salvation Army long ago, but Doug was a little different. He'd been away for so long that he had no way of knowing that Whitney hadn't turned into a slob while he'd been gone. She pulled on a pair of jeans that still fit her and a roomy top. She had no idea how she'd explain her sudden need to change clothes, but she'd worry about that when the time came.

She looked at herself one more time in the mirror and gasped. She'd forgotten all about her hair. What difference would it make that she'd changed her clothes if her hair still looked like it had been combed with an eggbeater? She pulled out the elastic band and brushed through it the best she could. In the end, the ridge in her hair that had been caused by drying in a ponytail made her put it back the way it was, but at least it looked a little bit bouncier and a whole lot neater.

When Whitney went out to meet Doug, she found him in her studio. He was studying the canvas she'd been working on that morning, his arms folded across his chest.

"What do you think?" she asked, walking up behind him.

"I think it's great. I love how you really captured the feeling of motion in the creek. But . . ." His voice trailed off, leaving the remainder of his thought hanging in midair.

"But . . . what?"

He glanced over at her and grinned. "I don't want to say something that'll make you mad. Remember, I've experienced your wrath."

She smiled and held up her hand in a pledge. "I promise not to get upset at your constructive criticism."

"Okay. It's just that, as beautiful as this picture is, it feels like it's missing something."

Once again, Doug had amazed her. "That's exactly what I thought. At first I thought maybe it just needed some color—"

He looked at her now-clean nose. "The lavender?"

"Right. But the more I looked at it, I realized that's not what's missing. What do you think?"

Doug held up his hands in surrender. "Sorry, I can't help you there. But I can hardly wait to see it when it's really finished."

She scowled at the canvas, feeling like the missing element was almost close enough to touch, if only she could figure out what it was. "Yeah, I can't wait either."

They went back out to the living room, and Whitney realized he hadn't made any comment about her changing clothes. She didn't know whether to be relieved that she didn't have to answer his questions or irked that he hadn't noticed.

"Is that how you always work?"

It took a moment for the fact that he was talking to her to register. "Excuse me?"

"From photo to canvas, I mean." Whitney stared at him blankly, and he continued on quickly. "Not that there's anything wrong with it. I'm just interested in the kind of work you do and the way you do it."

Finally it dawned on Whitney what he was saying and she was able to jump into the conversation that Doug had been having with himself. "Oh, I don't mind you asking. I guess I'm a little surprised though. I don't remember you ever being very interested in my work." Or anyone else's, for that matter, she thought.

"That was before. Now I'm interested. Really." They looked awkwardly at each other. "So, back to the original question. Do you always work like that?"

Whitney felt the tension that had begun to build fade away. "I've found it usually works better for me to have a point of reference. That's what the photos are. They're more to inspire me than to have something to copy."

He nodded thoughtfully, as if she'd just explained nuclear physics to him. "Is that what you were doing the other day?"

"Yeah, I was picture hunting." Her mouth twisted into a wry grin as she remembered the ones she'd taken before the mud mishap. "There were some really dandy photos on that roll of film before it met its demise."

"Oh, that reminds me." He reached into the deep pockets of his light canvas jacket and pulled out four rolls of fresh film. Handing them to her, he explained, "They couldn't save the one in the camera, so I thought I could at least replace it."

"Thank you, Doug. You've more than made up for the other day." Whitney smiled at him, and the smile he gave her in return warmed her down to her toes. They'd been so close once, even if it had been years ago. It was really a shame his first day home had been so rocky. Then she had a sudden brainstorm. "Go outside."

"What?" His look was one of pure confusion.

She pushed him toward the front door, explaining as they went. "We're going to pretend that you just got home today, and start over with a clean slate."

With her last word she shut the door in his face. It took him so long to respond, for a moment she was afraid he might have gotten the wrong idea and walked away. But finally she heard the sound of him bringing the knocker down sharply on the door, producing three staccato beats.

"Who is it?" She asked in a voice so sweet it fairly dripped honey.

From the other side of the door, Doug answered in the same sticky-sweet tone. "It's your long lost brother-in-law."

She flung the door open and greeted him with the broadest, most exaggerated smile she could muster. "Why, Doug Poulten, as I live and breathe! What brings you here?"

She could see him biting down on his lower lip to keep from laughing out loud. "Oh, I was just passing by, and I thought I'd say howdy."

He made a great show of tipping an imaginary hat. At that, any semblance of seriousness they'd been able to produce was broken and they both burst into laughter.

Whitney held onto the door frame with one hand and supported her stomach with the other, almost doubling over with laughter. Doug was laughing too, until she straightened up and looked at him.

Whitney noticed the change that came over Doug, saw how his smile faded, his eyes going from amused to intense. It had been years since she'd thought about how truly handsome Doug was.

Somewhere deep inside, Whitney felt something spark to life, like a small electric shock. And something in the way he looked at her told her that Doug had felt it too.

Doug looked away out of awkwardness.

Whitney laughed nervously.

"So . . ." Doug broke the silence. "I guess we can say we're friends again, huh?"

"Yeah, I guess we can."

"Well, I'd better get back. I promised Dad I'd help him out with some of the corrals. You know how those horses get. If there's one weak spot in the fence, they'll find it."

He was rambling again, but Whitney was glad for it. By the time he finished his speech about ornery horses breaking down fences, she'd been able to convince herself that she'd made too much of what had just passed between them. And as she watched him walk down the path that led back to his parents' house, she was telling herself that it had probably all been in her imagination anyhow.

CHAPTER 4

For as far back as Whitney could remember, the Poulten family had their own tradition of Saturday family breakfast. No matter what each of the family members had planned, they would gather together on Saturday morning first. During her teen years, Whitney had often been invited to join them, and it had become a regular event after she and Cliff were married. Even after Cliff's death, Whitney had continued the tradition, looking forward to those Saturdays even more than before. They represented normality, continuity, and the love of family. So she saw no reason this Saturday should be any different just because Doug was back home.

When she walked in the back door, she was greeted by the usual hubbub that accompanied every Saturday morning. Myra was busy in the kitchen, dancing between the refrigerator, stove, cabinets and oven. Sarah and Jeannie had already arrived and were flying between the kitchen and the dining area, carrying plates, dishes, glasses, and whatever else their mother directed them to. Meanwhile, Hank Poulten was the eye of the storm, sitting calmly at the table, a Zane Grey paperback beside his plate and a cup of coffee in his hand. The only thing that was out of place was Doug, who picked that moment to stumble out of the hallway.

He had obviously just woken up. His hair was disheveled, his jaw and cheeks were covered with a shadow of stubble, and he wore only boxers and a thin cotton undershirt. Whitney felt her breath catch in her throat. What was it about him that fascinated her so? She had an almost uncontrollable urge to walk over to him, smooth down his hair, run her fingers against the coarse hair on his cheek. Her thoughts were definitely not appropriate.

"What's all the commotion?" he asked, rubbing his eyes with the heels of his hands.

"Good morning, son," Myra sang out to him. "You haven't forgotten Saturday family breakfast, have you?"

Doug groaned.

Whitney couldn't keep silent any longer. "Can we take that as a 'yes'?"

At the sound of her voice Doug immediately dropped his hands from his face. He was now fully awake and looked mortified. "Whitney. Uh, hi. Didn't see you there. Excuse me." With that he turned and disappeared back down the hallway.

Whitney chuckled and turned back to Myra. "Anything I can help you with?"

"Oh no, dear," she answered with a wave of her hand. "The girls and I have it covered. You just go sit down."

Whitney knew better than to argue with her mother-in-law, so she took her usual seat next to Hank and poured herself a glass of orange juice. He looked up from his book long enough to say good morning and ask her how she was feeling. Then he was once again absorbed in the story he was reading. When Whitney had first met Hank, she'd been amazed at how he could become immersed in a book or magazine no matter how much noise and commotion was going on around him. Now it was just another part of everyday life. In fact, Whitney found it odd if there wasn't some kind of reading material somewhere near him at all times.

It didn't take long before the flurry of activity ceased. One by one, Sarah, Jeannie, and Myra carried the last of the plates of food to the table and sat down.

"There we go," Myra said with a contented sigh. "Now we're ready."

At the same time, Sarah and Jeannie pointed to the empty chair at the table.

Myra frowned, irked at herself for the oversight. "Well, we're almost ready."

Doug emerged from the fastest shower on record, grabbed a towel and began drying off vigorously. How could he have forgotten Saturday family breakfast? It had been a staple of his childhood, continuing through his teen years and beyond. In fact, when he had packed up all his things and driven off on a Friday night heading for certain fame and fortune, he'd left the note to his parents leaning against the sugar bowl on the table. He was sure his mother had found it in the morning before she started cooking family breakfast.

Now, the insensitivity of that gesture struck him full force. It was bad enough that he hadn't said good-bye, but he'd basically laughed in the face of their dearest family tradition. How must his mother have felt? She was always so excited about their special family time together, but Doug had ruined it.

None of them could have known at the time, but they would never again all sit down together as a family. First Doug had been gone, and now Cliff was dead. The realization of that fact shook Doug.

He dressed quickly and ran a comb through his hair. The other day, Whitney had called him an unthinking, self-centered jerk. And she had been right. Doug realized now how his actions had hurt his family. But that was part of why he'd come back in the first place. It was time for him to make amends and move on. He just hoped the damage he'd caused wasn't irreparable.

"Doug," his mother's voice came from down the hall. "Put

some speed on it, son. Breakfast is getting cold."

A moment later, Doug walked into the dining area, freshly shaved and dressed in jeans and a clean plaid work shirt. He hesitated for a moment, looking over the table. It was filled with plates of food, all emitting heavenly aromas. During the last few years, Doug had spent most of his nights either in hotel rooms or on the occasional cot set up in an empty stall. He'd started most days with a cup of strong black coffee and, if he was lucky, a Danish or piece of toast. To see so much food set out for one meal was a little overwhelming.

Hank gave his son a good-natured teasing. "Well, are you going to stand there looking at it all day, or do you think you might want to eat some of it?"

"Sorry," Doug answered. "There's just a lot of food."

"There's going to be a whole lot less in a minute," Hank replied. "Have a seat."

The only open chair was next to Whitney. Doug couldn't help but wonder if that had been Cliff's usual place at the table.

"Sorry to keep you all waiting," he said again as he sat beside her. "Guess I've got to get back into the swing of things."

Hank closed his book, marking his place with a folded napkin, and set it aside. "Let's pray," he said.

All around the table, each of his family members took the hands of those on either side of them. Yet another family tradition Doug had to get used to again. To his left was his mother, who took his hand with a smile and a gentle squeeze. On his right was Whitney. He paused for a moment, trying to read the look she was giving him. Then he took her hand that lay palm up on the table beside him. Her fingers curled around his, warm and smooth, enclosing his rough skin in gentle acceptance. As Hank said the blessing, Doug tried hard to concentrate on the words his father spoke, but it was no use. He was completely distracted by the delicate hand holding his.

"Amen."

Doug hoped Whitney hadn't noticed that it took him a split second too long to release her hand after the prayer was over. If she did, she made no indication of it. Instead she reached quickly for a bowl of scrambled eggs and began filling her plate.

The room was immediately filled with noise as they began passing around platters of food. Conversation at the breakfast table was always lively, but it seemed even more so now to Doug. Trying to get his mind off Whitney, he looked across the table at his sisters. Though they were twins, they'd always strived to keep their individuality. When they were babies, their mother had delighted in dressing them alike, but as soon as they were old enough to realize what was happening, they'd refused to go along with it. This morning, Jeannie was casual in blue jeans and a T-shirt, her blond hair pulled back in a no-nonsense ponytail. Sarah, on the other hand, was wearing a sundress, and Doug was pretty sure the only way her short shaggy haircut retained its shape was through the aid of lots of gel and hairspray.

"So, Jeannie," he asked, passing her a plate of fried potatoes, "what's going on with you?"

"Oh, just the same old thing," she said with a careless shrug. "Our business is going well."

Doug looked at her, waiting for more information. When he saw that none was coming, he asked, "Really? Who are you in business with?"

She looked at him as if he were stupid, then realized her mistake. "Sorry, bro. I forgot you're a little behind on current events." She elbowed Sarah who sat beside her. "Sarah and I started up a business of our own last year."

Sarah nodded, putting down the pitcher of juice. "We have our own Web site. It's called Seeing Double. It's totally dedicated to twins. Books, clothes, chat rooms, jewelry. If it's about twins, it's on our site."

It sounded like the kind of wild idea his sisters would come up with. "And you're making money at this?"

"You don't have to sound so skeptical," Jeannie responded, obviously annoyed with him. "As a matter of fact, yes, we do make money, but I won't bore you with the details."

"Now girls," Myra spoke up, stepping into her usual role as peacemaker, "I'm sure your brother didn't mean to insult you. He's just curious about what you do, isn't that right dear?" She turned to Doug, waiting for his answer.

"Of course," Doug agreed quickly. "I'm just interested in your lives, that's all."

Sarah glanced at Jeannie, then gave Doug a smile. "Well, we're interested in your life too, Doug. Now that you're retired from racing, what are your plans?"

"I've got a few irons in the fire," he answered evasively. "But nothing definite just yet."

Jeannie nodded. "I see." Her voice was sympathetic. "That explains why you've moved back in with the folks. It would be very hard to get your own place with no income to rely on."

Doug set down his knife and fork, glaring at his little sisters. He loved them to pieces, but they certainly could get under his skin. "I'm staying with Mom and Dad so I can help out around here until I decide exactly what I want to do. I could certainly afford to get my own place if I wanted to."

"Of course he could," Myra said. "But even if he did, I'd talk him out of it. Your brother's been gone for so long, it's nice to have him around the house again. Now," she turned to Whitney, determined to put an end to her children's bickering, "what are your plans for today?"

All eyes turned to Whitney. Like it or not, she realized that she was now the new center of attention. She dabbed at her mouth with a napkin and gave them a weak smile. "I'm going to hike around and see if I can replace some of the photos I lost the other day."

This immediately got Doug's attention. He didn't know if he liked the idea of Whitney wandering around by herself. "Are you sure that's a good idea?"

"Of course," she answered casually. "After all, you went to so much trouble to have my camera cleaned up, it would be a shame not to use it. And it's a beautiful day." She paused for a moment, as if weighing the next thing she was about to say. "If you're not too busy, maybe you'd like to come with me?"

Doug felt himself relax. "Absolutely." He felt much better knowing that if Whitney ran into any problems, he would be there to protect her.

"So this is how you find inspiration, huh?"

Whitney looked behind her and laughed. She knew Doug had been concerned about her tramping through the woods on her own, so she found it all the more comical that he was having a hard time keeping up with her.

"You never know what you'll find that will inspire you," she said with a smile and kept right on walking. "Or where you'll find it."

Whitney was still a bit surprised with herself for inviting Doug to come along. True, it was nice to have company again. Since Cliff's death, all her photo hunts had been solo. But it was odd that Doug was the one to be with her now. A week ago, he was the last person she wanted to see. Now her feelings of animosity toward him were gone, but she still had a lot of unanswered questions.

He ducked a low-hanging branch and walked up to her side. "The foliage is so thick here, I'm surprised you don't bring a machete along."

"What, and spoil nature? Never." She crooked her finger,

motioning for him to follow. "Come on. Just a little bit farther and you'll see why I brought you this way."

True to her word, they had gone only a few more yards when they came to the edge of a clearing. Whitney put her arm out to stop him from going ahead, then put a finger to her lips, signaling silence. Without a sound, the two stood there, looking out on a beautiful clearing. The creek flowed gently through it, while wild flowers and cattails grew on either side of its banks.

It was one of Whitney's favorite places. She could stand there for hours, just listening to the sounds of nature. If she was very still, it was as though all her senses became extra acute and she could feel when something was going to happen. Like now.

She sensed Doug before she felt him. He was leaning into her, his head coming closer and closer to the side of her neck. She should move away from him, but anticipation held her rooted to the spot. Soon, she could feel his breath against her cheek and feel the warmth of his lips against her ear.

"Why are we standing here?" he whispered.

The breath she'd been holding came out in a whoosh. She wasn't sure what she'd expected from him, but it hadn't been that. Once again, she put her finger to her lips. You'll see, she thought. If we're lucky.

And they were. About fifteen minutes after they'd arrived at the clearing, there was a rustling on the other side. Whitney nudged Doug carefully, motioning for him to look across the creek. A doe was stepping gingerly from the shadows of the trees, her eyes scanning the clearing and her ears swiveling like radar sensors. When she decided it was safe, she walked carefully to the water's edge, then lowered her head and began to drink. Whitney positioned her camera, watching the deer through the viewfinder. This would make up for the pictures she'd lost.

She was able to fire off several shots before the doe's head snapped up. Whether the wind had shifted or the doe had heard the soft whirring of the camera, Whitney would never know. The doe turned quickly and disappeared back into the relative safety of the thick growth of trees.

Whitney turned to Doug. "It's okay to talk now. Our position's been made."

He was smiling. "How did you know that would happen?"

"I didn't," she answered, walking to a fallen log near the water. "I just hoped it would. I found this spot a couple of years ago. I discovered that if I'm very quiet and the wind is with me, I can almost always catch a thirsty animal."

She sat down on the log and patted the rough bark beside her. "I need a rest. Have a seat if you'd like."

For the next few minutes they sat in companionable silence, just listening to the breeze rustle through the trees and the low gurgling of the creek. Once more, Whitney was aware of Doug, but not just in a physical way. Since the day he'd come home, she'd felt as though he was holding something back. It was as if he had things he wanted to say, but was afraid to. Now she felt as if he was on the brink of making some important disclosure, but couldn't quite make himself spit it out.

"So, do you come here often?"

Whitney laughed. Again, it wasn't what she'd expected, but at least he was talking.

"Quite often, actually," she answered. "Cliff and I used to come here." How this place has changed, she thought. It had started out as a special, secret place where she and Cliff had talked, and kissed, and held each other. Then it had become her place to grieve, away from the helpless attempts of well-meaning friends trying to console her. And finally, she'd made peace with God here, asking him to forgive her for doubting her faith.

Now she was here with Doug, and although the idea of it was strange, it wasn't unpleasant. "What about you?" she asked him. "Did you have a special place to go to over the past few years?"

Doug frowned and shook his head. "Nope. The life I led was very nomadic. We always had to move to the next race, the next track. The closest thing I had to a special place was whatever hotel bed I crashed in every night."

"Sounds grim," she said. "Can I ask you something?"

He looked wary, but nodded.

"Why did you leave home in the first place?"

"I wanted to train race horses," he said simply. "You know there wasn't a lot of opportunity here. I'd gone as far as I could go on the local circuit."

"I know, but why did you leave the way you did? It was so sudden. None of us knew you were leaving. You didn't even say good-bye to the family."

He leaned forward, elbows to knees, his hands clasped together. He was a big man, but it seemed to Whitney that he was trying to make himself as small as possible. Maybe that's how he felt.

"I've asked myself that a lot, especially lately," he finally said, "and I haven't come up with a great answer. I guess I thought nobody would care one way or the other."

Whitney was shocked. "How could you think that?"

"It just didn't seem like I belonged here anymore," Doug said with a shrug. "Everybody was moving on with their lives. Sarah and Jeannie were in college. You and Cliff had each other. The rest of my friends were either getting married or starting careers. I was a disappointment to Dad because I wouldn't join the family business." His voice trailed off and he looked at the water running down the creek and disappearing through the trees. "I just felt that if I didn't leave when I did, I was going to explode."

Whitney wanted to ask him why he hadn't at least kept in

touch, written occasionally or called, but Doug was through talking. He got to his feet, his face once more controlled and his feelings closed off.

He held his hand out to her. "Ready to head back?"

She took his hand and he helped her to her feet. Whitney was sure there was a whole lot more that Doug wasn't sharing with her, not only about his time away from the family, but why he'd decided to come back after all those years. She wanted to ask him more questions, but something told her it was better not to push. At least today he'd shared a little of what lay beneath the surface. Whitney knew that only time and patience would reveal the rest of Doug's hidden feelings.

CHAPTER 5

The knock on the door took Whitney by surprise.

Every Sunday, the Poulten's came by to pick Whitney up for church. Usually, Jeannie would burst in and call "Whitney! We're here!" Sometimes Myra would walk in quietly with a gentle, "Whitney, honey? Are you ready?" But no matter who came to get her, they'd always walk right in. No one ever knocked. In fact, the only time she could remember anyone knocking on the door was when Doug had stopped by.

That thought made her stop in her tracks, and she stood in front of the door, just staring at it. Doug? She shook her head sharply. No, it couldn't be him. Sure, he'd changed a lot, but this would be too much to ask for. He'd made it very clear as a teenager that he didn't enjoy participating in "organized religion." The older he got, the less and less he'd attended church, until finally he never went at all.

But when she opened the door, there he stood, his pale blue broadcloth shirt crisp and clean, and his silver and turquoise bolo tie sparkling. "Mornin', Whit. Are you ready?"

She tried hard to hide the astonishment that she felt. "Sure. Just give me a second."

She grabbed her purse, turned off a few lights, and went out to the gravel driveway where Doug waited for her, holding open the door of his pickup truck. "Where's everybody else?" she asked.

He grinned. "I'm just upsetting the balance of things all over.

Now that I'm back, there's not enough room for all of us in the sedan, so I offered to come get you and meet up with the family in town. I hope you don't mind."

"Oh no," Whitney answered quickly. "It just took me by surprise. I guess I'm a creature of habit."

"Well, you know what they say about change. It being good and all." He held out his hand and she looked at it for a moment before realizing that he was offering to help her into the truck. She grasped it as she stepped up, enjoying for a brief second the strength and support that it offered.

They chatted as he drove, and it seemed like no time at all had passed when they'd finished the thirty-minute trip into town. They pulled into the parking lot and met the rest of the Poulten family waiting for them in the small courtyard in front of the church.

Inside they greeted friends with hugs and handshakes. More than one woman came up to Whitney to ask her how she was feeling and to offer advice on everything from backaches to nausea. But what caused the most commotion was Doug's presence. The prodigal son had returned, and although some were ready to prepare him a feast, others looked like they'd just as soon cast him out.

Feeling a need to rescue him, Whitney tapped Doug on the shoulder. "The service is going to start soon. We'd better sit down." He flashed her a grateful smile, nodded, and followed her into the sanctuary.

Hank and Myra Poulten sat in the third pew from the front, on the right, just as they had for their entire married life. It was where all their children sat, where Whitney and Cliff had sat together, and where she now led Doug and sat down. Looking over at him, she was hit by a strange feeling. It was a mixture of how odd it was not to have Cliff beside her, but how right it was to see Doug there. She noticed that his eyes were closed and his head slightly bowed, as though he was preparing his heart for the service to come. Whitney looked away, ashamed of herself for intruding on such a personal moment.

It wasn't long before Pastor Rogers stepped up to the pulpit and the service began.

"Greetings to you in the name of the Lord!" he boomed heartily. "Please turn in your worship books to page sixty-three, 'This Is The Day That The Lord Has Made.' "

The worship team began to play, joining the clatter of the congregation rising to their feet and the rustle of pages as they searched for the song. Whitney and Doug reached for a book at the same time, their hands stopping just short of it. Whitney pulled her hand back, but Doug took the book, opened it to the right page, and held it between them. "Want to share?" he whispered.

Whitney nodded her agreement and they began to sing, he holding the left side of the book and she holding the right. It was a beautiful, uplifting song, one that Whitney had always loved. But it became a little more robust and earnest when she heard Doug belting it out next to her. Whitney couldn't help smiling to herself. What Doug lacked in vocal ability he more than made up for with enthusiasm.

As the final notes of the last verse died away, Pastor Rogers addressed the congregation once more. "Before you're seated, please greet your neighbors in the name of the Lord."

Whitney shook the hands of those all around her, smiling and exchanging niceties. When she turned to Doug, her heart broke a little for him. His hands were clasped in front of him, and he was trying not to look awkward. Whether deliberate or accidental, no one in front or behind had extended a hand to him, and since he sat on the aisle, she was the only member of the family next to him. Whitney felt a spark of indignation. Doug may have made mistakes in the past, but he definitely didn't deserve to be shunned.

She smiled broadly at him and thrust out her hand. "Good morning . . . again," she said with a chuckle.

Doug took her hand, but then surprised her by pulling her into a gentle hug. "Thank you, Whit." His words were warm and soft in her ear.

She had to pull back a little to reply. "I'm really glad that you're here, Doug."

They broke out of the embrace and sat down. And as the rest of the congregation did the same around them, Doug laid his hand on Whitney's and whispered, "I've been praying for you and the baby. You're very important to me." He gave her hand a quick squeeze and then pulled away.

It was all Whitney could do to drag her attention back to the service at hand. But no matter how hard she tried to stay focused, her mind kept going back to Doug. What had changed him so much? And why was she reacting so strongly to him?

"What about Noah's ark?"

Mary Ann Chambers, the petite brunette who was in charge of the church nursery, had corralled Whitney as soon as the service was over. A much-needed facelift was in the works for the nursery, and Mary Ann wasn't shy about asking for help. The two women stood in the church garden, discussing what subject would make the best mural.

"Noah's ark is nice," Whitney agreed. What she didn't say was that every church nursery within a five-hundred-mile radius probably had their own version of a Noah's ark mural. She didn't want to dampen Mary Ann's enthusiasm, but if she agreed to take on the project, she would have to come up with a different twist on the subject. "It certainly has a lot of potential. Why don't I put together some sketches, and then we'll see what you think?"

"Sounds great. Oh, excuse me," Mary Ann stood on her tiptoes, her eyes following the top of a battered tan cowboy hat as it moved through the crowd. "I see John Gillis over there. I've got to talk to him about building some cupboards. See you later!"

Whitney watched Mary Ann bound over to the side of the six-foot-plus rancher. Although he raised cattle for a living, John was well known for his carpentry skills. He was also quite handsome and very single. As soon as Mary Ann said hello, he took off his hat and leaned down ever so slightly to hear every word that she said. Whitney couldn't help but smile. There definitely seemed to be some sparks between those two.

Her stomach growled, chasing away all thoughts of anything but the fact that she'd had nothing to eat all day but two pieces of toast and a glass of juice. As if on cue, Jeannie ran up to her and asked if she was ready to go to lunch.

"Absolutely. Just let me find your brother." She scanned the thinning crowd that was assembled in the garden area, but didn't see him.

"Okay," Jeannie said, bouncing lightly on the balls of her feet. "I'll round up everybody else. We'll meet you there."

Whitney finally found Doug in the last place she looked—inside the sanctuary. He and Pastor Rogers were sitting in a pew, engrossed in conversation. She tried to back out without being noticed, but Doug looked up and spotted her.

"I'm sorry," she said quickly. "I didn't mean to interrupt."

Doug stood up and smiled broadly. "Don't go, Whitney. Pastor and I were just finishing up." He shook the hand of the man next to him. "Thanks for your time, Pastor Rogers."

"If you ever need to talk, Doug, my door is always open." He slapped the younger man soundly on the back. "It's good to have you home, son."

Doug didn't say much on the short ride to LeRoy's, the

restaurant that was a usual Sunday-after-church hangout for the Poulten family. He was uncharacteristically quiet all through lunch, although he did polish off a huge steak sandwich, home fries, and cherry pie à la mode. And even though he was very polite about helping Whitney into the pickup, all he said before they started driving was to buckle up. Whitney respected his privacy. Whatever he and Pastor had been talking about was evidently still very much on his mind. She looked out the passenger side window as they drove, trying hard not to obsess over what he might be thinking about, and failing miserably.

"Whitney."

The sound of his voice booming out her name in the cab made her jump.

He glanced at her quickly then turned back to the road. "Sorry. I didn't mean to startle you."

"You've just been so quiet ever since we left church. I wasn't expecting you to talk, I guess. What is it?"

He was silent for a moment, and Whitney thought he'd changed his mind about talking. But then he took a deep breath as if drawing in strength from some unseen force and the words slowly came out. "Well, like I told you in church, I've been praying for you and the baby this past week. And I've been thinking about you a lot since I came home."

Whitney watched as his fingers fiddled with the steering wheel. He always fidgeted when he was nervous. "That's sweet of you, Doug. I appreciate it."

"But I want to do more for you, Whitney. You shouldn't be alone at a time like this."

He was getting much too serious for her. "And what time is it?"

With an exasperated grunt he pulled over to the side of the road and stopped the truck short, making Whitney exceedingly glad that she had fastened her seatbelt. "I'm serious." He turned to face her. "You're a new widow about to be a new mother. You put up a brave front, but I know this can't be easy for you, so don't tell me it is."

"Okay," she said as lightly as possible. "I won't lie to you. Sometimes it's very hard. But I'm fine, Doug. You really don't need to be concerned about me."

"Yes, I do. I'm responsible for you."

She didn't believe she'd heard him right. "You're what?"

"I'm responsible for you," he repeated definitely. "And it's a responsibility that I don't take lightly."

Her eyes narrowed as the pieces of the puzzle started falling together. "Is this what you were talking to Pastor Rogers about?"

"Partly."

"I don't believe this. Of all the arrogant, conceited, egotistical—"

He looked at her, incredulous. "What?"

"I'm a big girl, Douglas Poulten, and I can take care of myself. I was just fine before you came home, and I'm just fine now. What makes you think that after all these years you can just waltz back into my life and claim responsibility?"

"The Bible."

His last comment made her do a doubletake. "What did you say?"

"The Bible makes me think I should take care of you . . . need to take care of you." She was ready to blast him again, but he held up one hand to cut her off. "Whitney, please, hear me out. Will you at least let me explain?"

She looked away from him, out the window at the wildflowers waving back and forth in the breeze, and counted to ten, forcing herself to calm down.

"All right," she finally answered from between clenched teeth. "Explain."

"The Bible says we need to look after widows and orphans—"

She cut him off. "I'm not an orphan."

"No," he conceded. "But you've never been all that close to your family. You haven't mentioned your mother once since I've been back."

Whitney didn't like the turn this conversation was taking. She and her mother had never been particularly close. While other mothers seemed content to help out at school and take care of their family, Whitney's mother had been driven to bigger things. She'd always worked, even when she didn't have to. As a real estate agent, her job consumed all of her days and many of her evenings. After Whitney's father left home, her mother had worked even harder, which was one of the reasons Whitney had hung out at the Poultens' so much. Whitney knew that not every woman was cut out for the traditional roles of wife and mother. In fact, she'd always thought her mother would make a great CEO. Whitney loved her mother, but she'd long ago resigned herself to the fact that they lived completely incompatible lives.

"My mother moved to Nevada a few years back. With her arthritis, it was getting harder and harder for her to handle Montana winters. But we call each other," she added defensively. "It's not like we never talk."

"What about your dad?" he asked gently. "Have you heard from him lately?"

She shrugged, not about to let on how she really felt about her father. "You know my dad. He sends a card at Christmas, and occasionally he remembers my birthday. I'm fine with it."

"So it's pretty safe to say neither of them will be helping you out much when the baby comes."

"No, they won't." She turned on him, ready to put an end to the topic. "But your parents are always there for me, and so are your sisters and, well, I do have other friends." At the moment, she couldn't think of a single person she would feel comfortable calling in the middle of the night if she needed help, but she wouldn't admit that to him. "So your concerns are unnecessary."

"I don't think so." He held up his hand before she could cut him off again. "But even if they are, that's not the only reason that I feel responsible for you." He ran a hand through his hair, frustration apparent on his face. "Haven't you wondered why I came back home in the first place?"

Of course she had. Yesterday by the creek she felt like he was on the verge of telling her, but then he'd shut down. Looking back out the window, she simply nodded.

"I came home because of Cliff."

Whitney whipped her head around to face Doug. "Cliff? Why?"

"Because I left things so badly between us. The month before I took off, I made sure that Cliff knew how little I appreciated anything he did. I thought he was weak because of his love of writing, his lack of athletic ability, . . . his faith." Doug looked down at his hands, clenching the steering wheel like some kind of life preserver. "He loved you so much, Whitney, and I even belittled that."

She'd known their relationship was strained, but hadn't realized just how broken it was until now. "What made you change your mind?" It was hard to talk past the thick lump that had formed in her throat.

"I had a mentor on the racing circuit. His name was Stan. He was about a hundred years old and ornery as they come. But inside that crusty old carcass was a kind heart. He took me under his wing, taught me everything he knew." Now Doug turned away from her, and soon she could tell from his controlled breathing that he was trying to keep his emotions in check. "The most important thing he taught me, though, was not to be like him."

"Not to?"

His shoulders rose in a humorless chuckle and he nodded his head. "He was all alone. No family, never married, all he had were the horses he cared for and the people he worked with. He always told me, 'Son, if you ever have a chance to snatch yourself a real life, don't let it get away.' "

"I'll bet he's thrilled that you came home."

Doug shook his head and turned back to her, his eyes filled with pain. "He never knew. He died a few months back."

"I'm so sorry, Doug." The words were horribly inadequate, she knew. They'd been said to her time and again after Cliff died and, though well meant, had done little to comfort her. It had been so hard for her to lose her husband. How horrible it must have been for Doug to lose someone so close to him and then find out about the death of his brother. Wanting to offer more than hollow words, she reached out and took his hand. "I really am sorry."

He nodded, and looking down at their joined hands, continued. "When I went to Stan's funeral, there were more flower arrangements there than you could imagine. Almost everybody in the racing business knew him or had worked with him at one time, and they all sent flowers, but—" his voice cracked and he cleared his throat. "But only about a dozen people showed up. It was the most pitiful thing I've ever seen. No one else there really loved him. And I realized while the pastor was saying a prayer that I had no idea if Stan believed in God or not. The Pastor thanked the Lord that Stan's spirit was with him in heaven, but, Whitney, . . . I'm not sure that it is."

She wanted to reassure him, to remind him that only God can see a man's heart, but she thought better of interrupting. It was important to let him finish.

"That's when I knew I had to make some big changes in my life. As much as I loved Stan, I didn't want my life to end the way his had. That night, I prayed for the first time in a long time. And a few weeks later, I decided to come home and mend fences with my family, but especially with Cliff. I finally realized why I'd looked down on him. It wasn't because I thought so little of him. It was because I saw all the things he had, and how solid his life was, and I was jealous." He took in a deep, ragged breath and held it for a moment, steadying himself before he let it out slowly. "That's why it's so important that I help you. I was too late to tell Cliff how much I loved him. But you're here, and Cliff's child is here. At least let me put that love into action by being here for you."

He finally looked up from their joined hands and looked into her face, and a part of the self-sufficient facade she'd built to keep others from helping her melted. Letting him be involved with her and the baby was probably the last tangible connection he'd have to Cliff. How could she deny him that? Especially when he was right. In large part, she was alone, and it would be a great relief to have someone to lean on every now and then.

Wordlessly, she nodded, and even as a smile lit up his face, she couldn't help but wonder what she'd just set in motion with that one small action.

CHAPTER 6

Whitney ran out of the bathroom clutching a large terry-cloth towel around her dripping wet torso, being careful not to slip on the hardwood floor. The phone continued its incessant ringing as she snatched up the receiver.

"Hello," she gasped.

On the other end, Doug's concerned voice answered her back.

"Whitney, are you okay? You sound out of breath. Why'd it take you so long to answer the phone?"

"Calm down, Doug. I'm fine. I'd just gotten out of the shower when you called. I had to run out to answer the phone." She glanced down at the puddle forming at her feet on the living room floor. "I'm drip drying even as we speak."

"Oh." The word came out sheepishly. "Well, I didn't mean to interrupt you. I was just getting ready to go into town, and I wondered if there was anything you needed."

"I've got to go into town today, myself." She held the receiver between her ear and shoulder while trying to get a more secure grip on the towel. "I've got a doctor's appointment this afternoon. Wait a minute," she said, suddenly suspicious. "Didn't I mention that to you yesterday?"

"You know, I think you did," he answered offhandedly. "So since we're both going in, why don't we go together?"

His request caught her by surprise. "Together? You and I?"

Doug laughed. "That's generally what together means. It's a long ride into town. I wouldn't mind having some company.

How about you?"

Whitney debated for a moment. It would be nice to let someone else do the driving, but at the same time, she didn't like the idea of becoming too dependent on him. "The company would be great," she hedged, "but what are you going to do while I'm seeing the doctor?"

"I'll wait for you. They do have a waiting room, don't they?"

"Of course they do. But I don't want to put you out . . ."

She heard him sigh into the phone. "Whitney, you can't be putting me out if I'm making the offer. I'm only going into town to pick up the mail and get some stuff at the market that Mom needs. I might as well do something productive while I'm there."

"And you call waiting in an obstetrician's office productive?"

"Well, it is full of women who are producing."

As bad as his joke was, she couldn't stop herself from laughing. He was wearing her down, despite her best efforts. Doug must have realized it, because he continued earnestly. "Look, I'll come with you to the doctor's if you'll come with me to the post office and the market. And then I'll take you to Bernie's for lunch."

The mention of Bernie's had nearly the same effect on Whitney as a ringing bell on a Pavlovian dog. It seemed like forever since she'd been in the old burger joint, but that hadn't dulled her memory of it. She'd been eating so sensibly ever since she found out she was pregnant that just the thought of one of Bernie's thick, juicy, and very fattening double cheeseburgers sounded heavenly. Leave it to Doug to come up with the one thing she couldn't say no to.

"You've got a deal," she answered after an extremely brief moment of hesitation. "Should I meet you at the house?"

"No," he answered quickly. "I'll come pick you up. Be right there."

"Doug, wait!"

But he'd hung up before she could inform him that she was nowhere near ready to go out. She toyed with the idea of calling him back, but knowing Doug he was undoubtedly out the door already. If she tried to catch him, his mother would probably be the one to answer. As much as she loved her mother-in-law, the last thing Whitney wanted was to get caught up in a conversation with Myra and have Doug walk into the house and find Whitney wrapped in a towel.

"This is already turning into a very interesting day," she muttered to herself as she trotted back down the hall to get dressed.

Ten minutes later, Doug stood at Whitney's front door, knocking but getting no answer. Finally he tried the doorknob. He didn't know whether to be pleased that it was unlocked so he could go inside, or to scold her for leaving herself accessible to any Tom, Dick, and Harry who might come by. Of course, not many dangerous strangers just happened to be ambling along in the woods of rural Montana, but there was always a first time. He'd probably scold her later, but for now, he'd let himself in and see what was taking so long.

When he walked into the living room, he understood why she hadn't heard him knocking on the door. The radio in her room was on, blaring some country western song about kisses being sweeter than wine. And, as if that weren't enough, the sound of a blow-dryer could be heard from behind the closed bathroom door.

Figuring he might have quite a wait ahead of him, Doug moved toward the couch to make himself comfortable. He was about to sit when he noticed the nearly dried puddle that had left a dark spot on the floor. So she hadn't been exaggerating. She really had been dripping wet when they talked on the phone. An image of Whitney fresh from the shower sprang into his mind. He could imagine her hair, hanging in wet auburn sections, dripping rivulets of water down her arms and pooling around her bare feet. He hoped she'd had time to grab a towel before she ran out of the bathroom.

Doug shook his head sharply. What was he thinking? This was his sister-in-law . . . his pregnant sister-in-law. He had no business thinking of how she might look after she got out of the shower, towel or no towel.

He sat down on the couch and let his head fall back against one of the cushions. He had to stop thinking about her this way. He'd been back home for a little over a week, yet he was thinking about her in ways he hadn't thought of any woman for a long, long time. And he was coming up with excuses to see her. Today was the perfect example. True, his mother had mentioned needing a few things the next time she went into town, but she hadn't asked Doug to go for her and she definitely hadn't said it was an emergency. But he'd remembered Whitney mentioning that she had a doctor's appointment and saw it as the perfect opportunity to make good on his pledge to be available when she needed help. So he'd used his mother's errand as an excuse to call her.

He tried not to think too hard about why he'd been so excited when she agreed to his idea. *I'm just being a good brother,* Doug thought. *Cliff would appreciate the fact that his wife wasn't driving to town and back alone. And the woman has to eat. Getting lunch for her is the least I can do.*

The house became a little quieter as the sound of the hair dryer ceased. Doug's head jerked up and he looked toward the hall. A sudden dread came over him. What if she wasn't dressed? She had no idea he was even in the house, so what would stop her from coming out in her underwear? Or worse. He should have let her know he was there. Or just waited outside until she answered the door, or . . .

This wasn't getting him anywhere. Compose yourself, he thought. There's absolutely nothing you can do about it now. Try and look nonchalant. He quickly picked up a magazine from the coffee table, flipped it open and balanced it on his leg.

Behind him, he heard the bathroom door open.

"Hi there!" he boomed without turning around.

He heard her gasp. Oh no.

"Doug. You startled me. I didn't know you were here."

He heard her walking toward him, and Doug finally relaxed. She wouldn't be coming anywhere near him if she weren't dressed. He turned to look at her and smiled.

"I rang the bell and knocked, but I guess you couldn't hear me. So I just let myself in. You know," he added with a smile, "this sort of thing wouldn't happen if you kept your door locked."

She nodded, but otherwise ignored his statement. "I'm sorry to keep you waiting."

"No problem," he said with a careless shrug. "I was just reading a magazine."

Whitney stood behind him, leaning over his shoulder to see what he'd been so absorbed in. "The Joys of Breast Feeding," she read. She looked at him sideways, a smirk on her face. "Yes, I'm sure you'd find that fascinating."

Doug looked down at the magazine. Bad enough he'd opened to that particular article, but to make matters worse there was a full-page photograph of a young mother with her infant nuzzled against her bare breast. Wonderful. Now Whitney would think he was a postnatal Peeping Tom.

He tried his best to sound unflustered when he answered her. "Well, I believe in keeping abreast of a variety of subjects."

"Obviously." Whitney giggled at his poor choice of words.

"I give up," he muttered, getting to his feet as he tossed the magazine back on the table. "So, are you ready to go?"

She bit her lip as though trying to hold back another smile. "Sure, just let me get my purse."

She went back into her room. The music ended abruptly and the house was completely silent. She came back through the living room, her purse slung over her shoulder, and he followed her out the front door. She was about to climb into the passenger's side of his pickup, when she turned to him, unable to resist one more comment.

"You probably will like the doctor's office after all. They've got lots of magazines in the waiting room."

Sitting in a booth at Bernie's, Whitney looked down at the cracked vinyl on the seat beneath her and thought of how little the place had changed. In fact, from the moment she and Doug walked through the door and her nostrils had been assaulted by the familiar smells of fried meat, onion rings, and milkshakes, Whitney felt as though she'd gone back in time. How many times had she, Cliff, and Doug sat in the very same booth as children? Coming to Bernie's had been a big thing back then, when they'd had to talk their parents into bringing them to town and dropping them off. Later, when they were in high school, Bernie's had been the spot to go after a game. Of course, during the one year they were all in high school at the same time, Doug had been one of the top players on the football team, so he always sat with the other jocks and their cheerleader friends. That was when Cliff and Whitney found themselves constantly pairing up. And before long, they'd been glad that Doug had other things to do.

Now, glancing at Doug over the top of a well-worn menu, Whitney couldn't help but think it felt a little strange to look across the beaten-up Formica tabletop and see his face instead of Cliff's.

Doug noticed her looking at him and smiled. "The old place

hasn't changed much, has it?"

Whitney smiled back, pulling her thoughts back to the present. "No, it hasn't. It's kind of like stepping into a time warp. I think Patsy still even works here."

As if to prove her point, a wiry, sixty-something waitress with brown curls as springy as steel wool approached their table, a broad grin on her long, thin face.

"Well, whatcha know. It's been a long time since I've seen either one of you." Her eyes narrowed and she leaned forward questioningly. "You didn't turn into vegetarians, did ya?"

"Absolutely not," Doug replied in mock horror. "I've been working out of state for the last few years. But just about as soon as I got home I had a powerful hankering for a Bernie's burger, so here I am. What's your excuse, Whitney?"

She kicked Doug under the table, but smiled sweetly at the waitress. "I've just been busy. I usually eat at home."

Patsy nodded briskly. "Well, I'm glad to see you came to your senses and got out for some real food. Now, what can I get you kids?"

They placed their orders, holding back their laughter until the waitress left their table.

"I don't remember the last time somebody called me a kid," Doug remarked.

"I guess the teenagers that used to hang out here will always be kids to Patsy." Whitney sighed at the thought of her teenage years. "Boy, life was simple back then."

"I guess it was. In retrospect, anyway."

She stared at him, surprised that retrospection was something that would even cross his mind. "Don't you think life was easier back then?"

"Well, sure," he said with a shrug, "but that's only because I know what I do now and I can look back at my teenage experiences with that perspective. But back when I was a teenager, well, that's a whole different story."

His smile faltered and he looked away, as though embarrassed by what he'd just said. But this new side of Doug intrigued Whitney. She wouldn't have expected him to give his teen years a second thought. "Would you care to expound on that?" she encouraged.

He looked directly at her, his warm brown eyes never wavering from hers. "That depends. Are you really interested?"

"Very."

He nodded. "Okay. Think back to when you were a teenager. Remember how new and intense everything was? It was like every emotion was multiplied a hundred times. You weren't just happy, you were euphoric. And you weren't sad. You were totally desolate. Back then, it actually felt like a matter of life and death whether our team won the homecoming game or you had a date to the dance. And there really was no such thing as a crush. No matter what anybody's parents call it, when teenagers fall in love, it's a real, all-encompassing emotion. Because, up to that point, that's the only way they know how to love—with every ounce of their being. Of course, the more often you fall in and out of love, the more jaded you become. But don't you remember the first time you looked at a boy and realized you loved him?"

Whitney's mind flashed back to her first day of high school, and she did remember. She remembered how she'd agonized over what to wear, and whether or not the backpack she'd stowed all her supplies in would be considered childish by her peers. She'd gone back and forth between taking lunch or buying it, and finally decided that buying lunch at the cafeteria would be the cooler thing to do. But most vividly of all, she remembered how Doug had smiled at her that day, in front of anybody who was there to notice, and said, "Welcome to the big time, Whit." At that moment, he'd grabbed her heart. He had been her first love, and she had loved him with an intensity and devotion that only a teenager can posses. He'd been in her thoughts night and day, and the most important thing in the world had been just to be around him or even merely to catch a glimpse of him. But how could she admit that to him now?

"Yes," she answered simply. "I remember."

He continued on, oblivious to the inner conflict Whitney was having. "Well, that's my point. I don't think life was any simpler then, not based on our frame of reference. Because do you remember when that first love ended? There's nothing simple about a pain like that."

Oh, she remembered when it had ended, all right. It was the day she'd realized that Doug would never see her as anything but a little sister. She'd thought the world had come to an end that day. But then Cliff had come into her life in a different way than he'd been in it before, and she'd experienced a love that was more complete than anything she'd ever known. Never had she regretted being with Cliff or wished that things might have been different. Never had she looked back and wished she could be with Doug instead. So it seemed strange to her that she and Doug would be having this conversation and dredging up old memories.

"You're right," she agreed. "The end of love is the hardest thing imaginable."

A kind of pall came over Doug and he passed his hand quickly across his face. "I'm so sorry, Whit. I can be so incredibly stupid sometimes."

Whitney shook her head in confusion. "What are you talking about?"

"Here I am going on and on, talking about first loves and love ending, and it didn't even hit me until just now. The last thing in the world I want to do is hurt you, but it seems like I keep on doing it."

And then she realized why he was so upset. He thought Cliff had been her first love. Whitney could feel the heat rushing to her cheeks and knew she must be turning an unbecoming shade of red. She wanted to reassure him, but how could she tell him the truth—that *he* had been her first love?

"Doug, it's okay. Really."

"No," he insisted. "I've got to learn to think before I open my big mouth. I—"

"Doug!" She reached out to grab his hand as it fiddled self-consciously with the silverware. "Doug, it's really okay. Cliff wasn't my first love."

The silence that fell at their table seemed to extend to the entire restaurant. Doug dropped the fork and looked sheepishly at Whitney.

"He wasn't?"

"No," she answered with a gentle smile. "He was my true love, but he wasn't the first."

"Oh."

Their eyes locked for one uncomfortable moment and then they looked away, glancing down and realizing simultaneously that what Whitney had meant as a gesture to silence Doug had digressed from its original purpose. Somehow, their fingers had intertwined and locked into something more intimate.

Whitney slowly pulled her hand from his, resisting the temptation to yank it away. "What surprises me," she said as evenly as possible, "is that you were in love in high school. I had no idea you and Shawna were so serious."

"I was serious," he said with a rough laugh, "but she wasn't. She dumped me right after I told her that I couldn't play football anymore."

"You've got to be kidding!" Whitney was furious at the idea of someone being so shallow. How could you claim to love somebody and then leave him just because he wasn't as athletic as he used to be?

There was no rancor in Doug's voice when he continued. "At least she was honest. She was desperate to get out of 'small-town hell' as she called it, and she figured I was her way out. When she found out there was no college scholarship for me, no chance at going pro, she figured it was time to cut her losses. Which just goes to prove my point."

Whitney cocked her head to one side. "I'm not following."

"I thought Shawna and I had something special, but now I see it for what it was. Now I realize that our relationship fulfilled a need each of us had, but it wasn't built on real love. I have no regrets now about the way things turned out, but at the time, it really did a number on me." Doug looked across the restaurant, shaking his head. When he looked back at Whitney, his eyes twinkled. "This has been some conversation, huh?"

"Not exactly what you'd expect from the two of us, is it?"

Before he had a chance to answer, Patsy approached their table carrying two plates piled high with food. Whitney was relieved by the distraction. She was glad Doug felt comfortable opening up to her, but she was afraid if they talked any longer, he would press the issue and want to know who her first love had been. That was a revelation she wasn't ready to make. They got down to the business of eating, once more comfortable in their silence.

"Oh," Doug finally said between bites, "I have more news."

Whitney grinned. "Are we going to psychoanalyze something else?"

Doug groaned. "No, it's about Dad. You remember how he always used to talk about me taking over the family business one day?"

"Sure." Hank Poulten had been a packer most of his adult life. He arranged and led hunting trips for well-to-do business-men who wanted to rough it out in the wilderness. It was a profession he loved, and he had tried to instill that love into his oldest son every chance he got. "I also remember you were adamantly opposed to the idea."

Doug nodded. "Well, believe it or not, I've changed my mind."

Whitney stared at him in amazement, the cheeseburger that she was holding poised halfway between the plate and her mouth. "You can't be serious."

"I am," he answered with a smile. "And be careful, your tomato is about ready to slide out of your burger."

She looked down at her hands. Sure enough, her slippery burger was coming apart and was ready to fall to her plate in pieces. She set it down, wiped off her hands, and took a sip of her lemonade. "So, let me see if I've got this straight. You're giving up the glamorous, fast-paced world of Thoroughbred racing so you can spend half of the year living in a tent in the woods with a bunch of greenhorns who don't know which end of the rifle is up?"

Doug wiped a stray drop of ketchup off his chin. "Not exactly. I am leaving the racing game to go into business with Dad, but we're going to change the emphasis. It's been pretty hard for him to make ends meet lately."

She was well aware of how tight things had been for her in-laws. The latest wave of political correctness had rendered hunting somewhat unfashionable, resulting in a steady decline in Hank Poulten's clientele. If it weren't for a handful of longtime customers who returned to him year after year, he'd already be out of business. "So what are you going to do?"

"We're going to operate a full-fledged horse breeding farm."

Whitney couldn't help but be impressed. "Are you going to breed Thoroughbreds?"

Doug shook his head as he swirled a french fry through a glob of ketchup. "No. Quarter horses, mostly. Sturdy work horses and horses for shows or rodeos. But I'm also going to indulge myself and breed Arabians." His eyes sparkled as he told Whitney about his fascination with the breed. "When you look at an Arabian horse, the first thing you see is a very delicate, fine-boned animal. They almost look fragile. But they're really one of the strongest, toughest breeds around. Most people don't realize it, but every Thoroughbred can be traced back to one of three Arabian foundation sires. In fact—" Doug stopped in midsentence. "Sorry. When I get on this topic, I tend to get carried away."

"Don't apologize," she said to him with a gentle smile. "I'm really interested. Tell me more."

As he did, she listened intently, watching him become more and more excited. His expression was positively animated and his eyes came alive. This was something that was important to Doug, and he was sharing it with her. She was glad. And as she ate the last of her burger, she realized how truly happy she was that he was home.

CHAPTER 7

"Mom, I've got your groceries!"

Doug closed the door behind him with his foot and carried the three full bags into the kitchen. Myra came around the corner from the living room, a smile on her face.

"Didn't you bring Whitney with you?" she asked, looking past him at the closed door.

Doug shook his head. "No, she was tired, so I took her straight home. Where do you want these?"

"Just over here." Myra pointed to the counter by the sink. She helped Doug set down his load, then gave him a kiss on the cheek. "Thank you so much for getting these things for me. It's nice to have you home again, and not just so you can run errands."

"It's good to be home too." He reached into the nearest grocery bag and pulled out a thick stack of envelopes held together with a rubber band. "And it's a good thing someone around here doesn't mind running errands," he said, handing the mail to her. "Doesn't Dad ever go to the post office?"

"Of course he does," she answered, giving him a playful swat. "He's just had a lot on his mind lately. By the way, your sisters are coming over for dinner."

Doug rolled his eyes. "In that case, I'm going to go outside and enjoy some peace and quiet while I can." He hurried out the back door before his mother could say anything else to him.

Once outside, he slowed his steps and dropped the happy

facade. There was one piece of mail that he'd left in his truck, and he knew he wanted to be alone when he opened it.

Doug pulled the thick manila envelope out from under his front seat and stared down at it. The return address was from the stable that had been his home base for the last year. As soon as he'd taken it out of the post office box, he knew what it was. Thankfully, Whitney had been engrossed in conversation with the postal clerk, so he'd been able to take it out to the truck and conceal it without her knowing. She had enough on her mind right now without him bringing up even more unpleasant memories.

He went down the path behind the house, but instead of going toward Whitney's as usual, he turned and went the other way. He hadn't gone far before he reached his destination. Looking up into the branches of the huge oak, Doug could see that the old tree house was still there. The boards looked a little more weathered, and the formerly bright-red curtains in the window had faded to a pale brown, but otherwise, it looked pretty much the same.

By the time he climbed up the rickety ladder and pulled himself through the hole in the floor, Doug was breathing hard, but not from exertion. He thought back to his childhood, remembering how he and Cliff would race each other to see who could get into the "fort" first. When they were younger, they'd pretended they were in a wilderness fort, protecting the settlement from savages. As they grew, their focus shifted from fantasy games to more pressing issues, like school, girls, and friends. But they continued to use the tree house as a place to be alone or to share important information with each other.

As soon as Doug had seen the envelope, he knew this was where he wanted to open it: in the place where he and Cliff had shared their deepest secrets with each other.

Sliding his finger under the lip, Doug opened the envelope

and spilled the contents out on the floor in front of him. On top of the pile was a short letter composed on Sunnydale Stable stationery. It had been computer written and was signed in neat handwriting that Doug didn't recognize.

"Dear Mr. Poulten," it started, "Please accept my apologies for the delay in getting these letters to you. I came across them while straightening up the mess left by the previous office manager."

Finally, the mystery of the missing letters was solved. They lay there in front of him, spread out on the rough wood floor, taunting him. It was bad enough his family had had to mourn Cliff, but at the same time they'd had to deal with the pain of thinking that Doug didn't care. If he'd received the letters sooner, things would have been so different. Doug sighed heavily. How could one person's carelessness result in so much sadness?

Slowly he reached out and picked up the letter with Whitney's return address. He hesitated, not sure he wanted to do this. "What difference will it make now?" he asked out loud. "I already know what they say." But then he couldn't stop himself. He needed to read these letters.

Whitney's began with the sentence, "I'm sorry to have to tell you this in such an impersonal way, but I don't know how else to get hold of you." It went on to tell him about the plane crash and that they were waiting as long as they could to have the funeral service in order to give Doug time to be there. "I hope you can come out," the letter concluded. "I know it would mean a lot to Cliff."

One by one, he opened the letters from his mother, Jeannie, and Sarah. They all pretty much said the same thing: We're sorry to have to tell you this way, but Cliff is dead and we hope you'll be home for the service.

Doug leaned back against the wall, and the whole tree house

groaned, as if it too was mourning the loss of Cliff.

"Why was I so selfish?" Doug asked himself. If only he'd called home once in a while, he would have known about the accident. At least then he could have been there to pay his last respects to his brother and support Whitney and the rest of the family.

He looked down at the remaining pile of mail. What was left appeared to be mostly junk mail and promotional items. But then, sticking out from the bottom of it all, he noticed the handwritten return address on the corner of a cream-colored envelope. The only part of it he could make out was the sender's first name, but it was enough to send a chill through him: Cliff.

Quickly he pushed the other mail aside as if the letter he sought might disappear if he didn't act soon enough. When he held it in his hand, he kept staring at it, trying to convince himself that it was really from his brother. But it was. From the postmark, it looked like Cliff had sent it just about a week before the accident.

Doug opened the envelope slowly, taking care not to rip it. It was important to him to treat this, the last thing his brother had sent him, with respect. Then he pulled out the letter. Doug looked down at the page, written in Cliff's painstakingly neat handwriting, and felt tears well up in his eyes. How he had longed for one more chance to talk to Cliff, and here it was. It was as if God had heard his prayer before he'd even had a chance to pray it.

Doug closed his eyes, taking a moment to send up a silent prayer of thanks, and then read the letter.

Dear Doug,

It's been such a long time, I hardly know where to start. You'd think that being a writer, I wouldn't be at a loss for words, but I am. I've just been thinking about you a lot over the last few weeks, and I knew it was time to write to you.

We weren't on the best of terms when you left, and I want to apologize for that. I'm not totally sure what caused the rift between us, but I know I could have done more to repair it. I just want you to know that, no matter what, I love you, and I always have.

I also hope that, somewhere along the way, you've let God back into your heart. There have been trials in my life that I couldn't have faced without the Lord to depend on. And not a day goes by that I don't thank him for bringing Whitney into my life. I'm a blessed man, bro. The only thing that would make my life better is knowing that, one day, when we leave this earth, you and I will see each other in heaven.

The last few lines of the letter were about their parents and their sisters, but they all blurred together. Doug let the letter fall from his hands and watched it waft gently to the floor. Had Cliff known? Somehow, had he known in his spirit how little time he had left? Why else, after so many years, had he suddenly needed to communicate these things to Doug?

Doug felt as though he were being assaulted by a barrage of different emotions. On one hand, he felt more peace in his heart than he had for quite some time. He knew his brother loved him and had forgiven him for the distance in their relationship. And he was reminded again of the fact he knew with absolute certainty: at that very moment, Cliff was in paradise with the Lord.

But then there was Whitney. Doug had always known that Cliff loved her with his whole heart. In fact, that had been part of the problem between the brothers. Not that Doug had wanted Whitney herself, but he'd yearned for a loving relationship of his own. As Doug had watched Cliff and Whitney grow closer, he had felt more and more left out and alone. Not only did he lack a partner to share things with, but he had to watch the brother who had always been his closest friend drifting away from him. All you had to do was see Whitney and Cliff together to know they were each other's best friend.

Which made his current situation all the more difficult. Since he'd come home, he'd been consumed with thoughts of Whitney and the baby. He'd even started making up excuses to see her. How could he reconcile the feelings he'd been having, especially after reading Cliff's letter?

"Doug!"

It took a moment for Doug to realize that a female voice was calling out his name. But when a rock sailed through the window, barely missing his head, he got the point. Pulling back the ragged curtain, he looked down to see Whitney standing at the base of the tree, her hands on her hips. She was the last person he expected to see.

"What are you doing here?" he called down. "I thought you were going to take a nap."

She looked up at him and shrugged. "I got a second wind. It happens on occasion. What are you doing up in the fort?"

Doug couldn't help but smile. "How did you know about this place?"

She waved a finger at him. "You didn't think you could keep a secret like this from me forever, did you? I've known about it since we were small, but I never wanted to intrude on your secret domain. What are you doing up there?"

"Just thinking," Doug hedged. "I'll be down in a little while."

Whitney shook her head. "Come down now."

"Why?"

"Because I want to talk to you, and I'm tired of yelling. Besides, I'm getting a crick in my neck from looking up." To emphasize her point, she made a face and rubbed her neck.

Doug looked at the letters strewn all over the floor. He needed to get rid of all this stuff so she wouldn't see it. "Okay. Just a few more minutes."

Whitney shook her head. "I didn't want to do this, but you're giving me no choice. Here I come."

Doug watched her walk toward the wooden ladder. She wouldn't really try to climb up that thing, would she? In her condition? But then she put her foot on the lowest rung, and Doug saw that she would.

"Wait!" he called down. "I'll come right down. Just step away from the tree."

With a laugh, she backed off, hands in the air as if surrendering. Quickly, Doug scooped all the letters together and shoved them into the envelope. Then he stowed them inside his jacket and made his way down the ladder.

When he was finally standing in front of Whitney, he frowned and tried to sound as stern as possible. "You are one crazy lady, do you know that? How did you even know where to find me?"

"I figured this is where you'd want to go to read the letters."

Doug felt himself blanch. "The letters?"

"Yes, the letters." Whitney's face softened and she put her hand on his arm. "I know you got a fat envelope from a stable today. I figured the lost letters had finally tracked you down."

"But how did you know?" Doug stammered. "I didn't think you even saw the envelope. You were so busy talking to the clerk."

She smiled gently. "What do you think we were talking about?"

Of course, Doug thought. One of the disadvantages of small-town life was that everybody knew your business and thought that anybody who didn't know it should. "I guess I should have known better than to try to hide it from you."

Whitney nodded, but didn't call him on it. "So, I guess you

got all the letters from the family."

"Yes."

"And I guess you must have got Cliff's letter too."

Again, Doug was taken by surprise. "You knew about the letter from Cliff?"

"Yep," she said softly. "I figured if you'd received it before, you would have mentioned it. It was a great letter."

"So, you knew what it said?"

"He asked me to read it before he mailed it. He agonized over that letter . . . went through several drafts, in fact."

Whitney was quiet for a moment. Doug could only imagine what she must be feeling, what she must be remembering, which is why Doug hadn't wanted to tell her about the letters in the first place. But then she asked, "Are you okay?"

Once more, Whitney was putting his feelings ahead of her own. "I don't know if I'd call it okay," he answered slowly. "I'm frustrated that I didn't get these letters sooner. I'm mad at myself for not calling Cliff when I had the chance." He stopped for a moment, pulling the envelope out of his jacket. "But mostly, I'm thankful that God heard my prayer before I prayed it. He gave me one last message from my brother."

A tear escaped the corner of Whitney's eye, but she brushed it away quickly. "Yeah, God's good at that. He gave me one last message too." Then she put her hand gently on her stomach, and the smile returned to her face.

CHAPTER 8

"I appreciate the thought, Gail, but right now I just can't."

Whitney drew her knees up on the couch and shifted the phone receiver from one hand to the other. Gail had been Whitney's agent since she had begun illustrating and, as a rule, Whitney trusted her judgment implicitly. But she hadn't been prepared for Gail's phone call, or for her request.

"I understand," Gail said. "But this opportunity came up, and I think it's perfect for you. You've got so much talent, I just hate to think of you sitting around doing nothing, letting it go to waste."

"You should know me well enough to know that I'm not just sitting around. I've been working on my painting. In fact, I've completed several canvases." And I'm in the middle of one canvas that I can't finish to save my life, Whitney thought with a frown.

"That's great." Gail paused, then continued hopefully. "Then maybe it wouldn't be such a stretch for you to consider working with this new author."

"Gail. No." Whitney was firm on this point. She knew Gail wanted to help her move on, and it touched Whitney that she would be so concerned about her. What Gail didn't understand, couldn't understand, was what a huge step it would be for Whitney to work with another author. Cliff was the only person she'd ever collaborated with. In a way, their work had been an extension of their marriage. To blithely move on and work with someone else just didn't feel right. It would be almost like having an affair.

"I'm sorry for pushing you, Whitney. I just hoped I could do something to help you. It's the least I can do." Gail's voice shook a little, which was totally out of character for the strong, independent businesswoman Whitney had come to know.

"What do you mean?"

Gail took a ragged breath before continuing. "If you must know, I feel partly to blame for Cliff's death."

Whitney shook her head, not sure she'd heard right. "You? How can you think that? Gail, you didn't have anything to do with it."

"Oh, yes, I did," she replied strongly. "It was my idea to have Cliff fly to New York and press the flesh at the publishing house. If not for that—" Gail's voice faltered, her sentence left unfinished.

Whitney took a deep breath. God deliver me from well-meaning friends with misplaced guilt, she thought. "Gail, listen to me. You had absolutely nothing to do with Cliff's death. Yes, you set up the New York meeting, but it was something he was excited about. He wanted to make the trip. Besides, I made his flight arrangements. I'm the one who booked him on that light plane for the last leg of the trip. Do you think that makes me responsible?"

"No," Gail replied in horror. "Never. Whitney, I'm so sorry. I never meant to imply—"

"I know," Whitney cut her off gently. "I just want you to understand how ridiculous it is to blame yourself. It won't bring Cliff back, and it doesn't help me. Just be my agent and my friend, and understand that I need a little more time before I take on any new projects. Okay?"

"All right. You just make sure you call me when you're ready to get back to work."

Gail's voice was crisp and businesslike again. Whitney knew they were back on the right track.

After she hung up the phone, Whitney stayed on the couch, her arms wrapped around her bent knees. The conversation with Gail had dredged up some unpleasant memories. There was a time when Whitney had thought herself responsible for Cliff's death. And not just partly, but completely and solely. It was one of the many things she'd had to make peace with in the weeks after the accident. Now, of course, she knew better and she had stopped blaming herself. She'd released herself from the guilt, but the pain of missing her husband was a lot harder to get rid of.

Whitney didn't know why, but an image of Doug darted into her mind. It had been two months since he'd made his promise to help her and be there for her. He'd been good to his word too. He called almost daily to check up on her, he picked her up every Sunday for church, and from time to time she ran into him while she was out walking in the woods. It made her wonder if he patrolled the area on the off chance that he'd run into her.

On one hand, Whitney bristled at the thought of being watched so closely, being treated as though she couldn't take care of herself. The last thing she wanted was to become a burden to anybody, especially someone as independent as Doug. More often, though, she was glad to know that somebody was looking out for her. She knew that if she ever needed something, all she had to do was call him. It made her feel safe, cared for, . . . even loved.

Whitney got up quickly from the couch and went into the kitchen. Well, of course he loves me, she thought, getting a glass from the cupboard. He's my brother-in-law. He's only doing what any brother-in-law would do.

But as she poured water into the glass, she couldn't help but think of the times when his look had been a little too intense.

Times when, in return, she'd felt anything but sisterly toward him. Was it possible that she was misreading him? Was she leaning on him too much, becoming too dependent on him? The thought nagged at her, even as she walked outside, wondering all the while what he was doing at that very moment.

The air was cool and a gentle breeze blew as Doug rode Apache, one of his father's horses, down the fence line. Even though Hank hadn't fully committed to changing the emphasis of his business, Doug knew there was too much work that needed to be done around the place to wait. He was counting on the fact that his father would eventually come around. In the meantime, Doug had called some of the folks he used to work with on the race circuit, trying to line up investors. He'd found out who the best local contacts were for feed, hay, and other necessities. And he'd worked on the stalls, the barn, and anything else on the property that needed fixing. Like the fence line.

In reality, it was one of the more relaxing things Doug had done since he'd been back home. Apache was an old quarter horse with an easy, rolling gait. He didn't just walk; he sauntered. Doug patted the horse's neck while keeping his eye on the fence. Hank had kept things around the ranch in pretty good shape, but Doug knew it was easy to miss a break or weak spot in the fence. Once they got some new stock at the ranch, he didn't want to see their investment skip out on them in the middle of the night.

Half an hour later, after flagging the portions of the fence he would need to come back and fix later, Doug turned Apache toward the barn. The horse's ears swiveled forward and his pace quickened. He obviously knew they were getting close to home and a bucket of oats.

Doug smiled. "We're not done yet, fella," he said in a low, soothing voice. "We've got one more stop before you can turn in for the day."

He pulled the reins against the side of Apache's neck, turning him away from the barn. Reluctantly, the gelding changed his course, but he communicated his displeasure with Doug by slowing his gait and dropping his head. In a moment they had gone behind the ranch house and down the trail that led to Whitney's.

In the months that Doug had been home, they'd seen each other almost every day. Even though he knew she was fine and probably didn't need anything from him, he felt drawn to her home. He knew Whitney wasn't crazy about him being around all the time, but he didn't do it just for her. Doug knew there was no way he could explain how much he needed those times with her. She was in his thoughts all the time, and though he tried to fool himself into thinking he was merely showing brotherly concern, deep down he knew it was more.

Doug squeezed Apache's sides with his knees, encouraging the horse to pick up the pace. Doug thought of the women he'd gone out with while he was away from home. There had been several, although none of them had made much of an impact. Oh, they were nice enough, and they were usually drop-dead gorgeous. One thing about running with a rich crowd was that they could afford to keep themselves looking their best, and they always did. But despite all the outward trappings, Doug had never met anyone who captured his heart. He realized now that he had never met a truly beautiful soul. Not before Whitney.

The horse rounded a corner and Whitney's home came into view. Doug was surprised to see that she was sitting on the front step, scowling at him.

He pulled Apache to a stop and dismounted quickly. "Whitney, is something wrong? What are you doing sitting out here?"

She squinted up at him, shading her eyes with one hand. "I

just figured if I sat outside long enough, you'd show up."

He wasn't sure how to read her. Either he had become a pest, or she was teasing him. "Would you like me to leave?"

She shook her head and smiled. "No. Now that you're here, you might as well stay a while."

"So," he said, joining her on the step, "anything interesting going on today?"

She looked over at Apache, who was casually munching the ground cover along the edge of the path. "My agent called."

"Really. Was it a good call?"

Whitney shrugged. "It's good to know my work is still in demand. But she wants me to collaborate with another author."

"And that's bad?" Doug asked, trying to fill in the spots that Whitney was leaving empty.

She nodded, spreading her hands out in front of her. The afternoon sun shone on the one small diamond in her wedding band, throwing splashes of light in every direction. "No matter how hard I try, I can't seem to get used to the idea of working with someone else." She paused, and when she spoke again her voice was low, almost a whisper. "It feels like I'd be cheating on him."

Doug felt as though someone had thrown cold water in his face. This was the thing he tended to lose sight of when he thought of Whitney. She was his brother's wife. If just working with a different author made her feel this way, how would she feel if she knew the thoughts he'd been having about her?

Doug struggled for something supportive to say. "I'm sure if you explain it to her, she'll understand."

"Oh, she does," Whitney assured him. "I just don't like feeling this way, you know?"

He nodded. They sat silently together, Doug trying not to acknowledge how aware he was of her physical closeness.

"But enough of that," she chirped, obviously determined to

brighten her mood. "The real reason I was sitting out here is because I was hoping you'd come by. I have a favor to ask you."

Again, Doug was caught off guard. Whitney wasn't in the habit of asking for help. "Sure. Anything you need."

Whitney grinned and held up a finger. "Don't be so quick to offer your services. You don't know what it is yet." Then her expression sobered. "Actually, it's a pretty big thing to ask."

Doug became equally serious. "Whitney, you know that whatever you need, you can count on me. Now, what is it?"

She took a deep breath and then blurted out, "I'd like you to be my childbirth coach."

That was definitely not what Doug had expected. *I need helping assembling the crib,* or, *I need you to go into town and pick up feminine products*—those kinds of things he could handle. But this request blindsided him. His expression must have shown it too, because Whitney quickly took it back.

"Never mind. See? I knew I shouldn't have asked. It's too big."

He looked at her, this woman who claimed to be so fiercely independent, and his heart melted a little. He thought of Cliff, and of his determination not to betray his brother's memory by getting too close to his wife. Doug knew being her childbirth coach would only draw him closer to her. But this was the first thing she'd actually asked of him, and there was no way he would let her down.

She was still chattering and gesticulating wildly, as if trying to erase her words from the air. Doug grabbed one of her hands and put a finger to her lips. She immediately became silent, her eyes wide and wondering.

"Of course I'll be your coach," he said with more confidence than he felt. Then to put her at ease, he grinned and said, "How hard could it be?"

CHAPTER 9

Once, early in his career as a trainer, Doug had seen a jockey fall from a horse during a race. The man had gone down into the middle of a pack of tightly jammed bodies and pounding hooves. After the field of horses moved on, the dust cleared and the jockey lay motionless in the dirt. He later found out that, miraculously, the jockey was only mildly injured, but at that moment, Doug had felt more fear than any other time in his life.

Until now.

He sat beside Whitney in a dark room full of expectant mothers and their partners. On a large screen in front of them played a film about the "miracle of birth." Doug had found the first part of the presentation, about conception and the formation and growth of the baby, fascinating. But now they had come to the part that showed the actual birth. It might be a miracle, but there certainly was a lot of pain involved. Not to mention blood.

The childbirth instructor's rapturous voice interrupted the movie's classical soundtrack. "Here comes the baby's head!"

The room was filled with murmured oohs and ahs. Doug glanced at Whitney. In the flickering light from the film, she smiled, captivated by the image in front of her. Doug simply felt queasy.

She must have felt his eyes on her because she turned to look at him. Her brow creased in concern and he knew he looked as bad as he felt.

"Are you okay?" she whispered.

He just nodded.

Her frown turned into a grin. "You're not thinking of backing out on me, are you?"

He shook his head.

She gave his knee a quick pat. "Good. Because I have no choice in the matter. We're in this together, buddy."

We're in this together. The words touched Doug. He liked the thought of them working together, having Whitney rely on him and being strong for her in return. He swallowed, shaking off his queasiness, and made himself return her smile. "Absolutely."

The film came to an abrupt end, and Janet, the instructor, flicked the lights back on. "All right now," she called out. "Everyone grab your pillow and find a spot on the floor. Time for some relaxation techniques."

Doug picked up the plump pillow beside his chair and followed Whitney to a large open room. Following the example of those around him, he helped Whitney to the floor, then sat cross-legged beside her.

Janet stood in front of the group. "Partners, sit with your legs apart forming a V. Expectant mommies, please sit in front of your partner with your back against his chest."

Of the dozen pregnant women, Whitney was the only one to hesitate. She turned to Doug, concern clear on her face. "Are you sure you want to do this?"

Obviously she had finally realized they were going to have close physical contact, and the idea gave her pause. As unsure as he was, Doug also knew this was important for her and the baby. It was up to him to put her at ease. "Hey, you had your chance to get rid of me," he answered lightly. "Now you're stuck with me for the duration."

She looked away, biting her lip. "It's just . . ."

He put one finger under her chin and turned her face till they were eye to eye. "I know. It's a little scary for me too. But what's most important is to do everything we can so that you have a healthy baby. I want to be here, Whit. I'm not going anywhere."

A look of relief filled her eyes. She nodded, turned her back, and leaned against him.

For the next fifteen minutes, Janet drilled them on breathing and focusing. Doug's face looked over Whitney's shoulder, and he breathed in the sweet scent of her hair that was brushing softly against his cheek. He could feel her intake of breath, and he realized they were breathing in unison. Of course, that was the whole point of the exercise, but to really experience it . . . for some reason, it created an even greater feeling of intimacy than he'd expected. He let his breath out slowly, and she did the same. His next breath in was deeper and a little shaky. Get a grip, he told himself. This is your brother's widow. What you're feeling isn't allowed.

The exercise finally came to a close. Please Lord, Doug prayed silently, let the class be over. But perky Janet was once again directing them. "Now for the fun part. Ladies, on your sides please, with your backs to your partners. Gentlemen, there's a lot of muscle tension that can accompany pregnancy, especially in the lower back. This massage technique is a great way to combat that."

Doug concentrated very hard on following the exact directions that Janet was giving. If he could keep focused on what he was doing, perhaps he could ignore how he was feeling.

Janet walked among the couples, checking to see that everyone had gotten the hang of it. When she came to them, she stopped and crouched down. "You're doing a great job, Doug. But go down a little farther."

Doug's hands had been hovering around the middle of

Whitney's spine, which he considered to be a safe spot. But now, prompted by Janet, his hands continued to knead her muscles, working down vertebrae by vertebrae until his fingers moved in small, tight circles at the small of her back.

"Perfect," Janet said with a smile. "How does that feel, Whitney?"

"Wonderful," Whitney replied dreamily. "In fact, I think I might fall asleep in a minute."

Janet laughed. "That's the point. You know, this is a really good exercise to do right before bed, for just that reason." She got up and walked on to the next couple.

"Doug?"

Whitney's voice was almost a whisper, so he leaned in closer to hear her. "Hmm?"

"Thank you." Her breath was warm against his cheek. "I don't know when I've felt this relaxed."

It was one more thread pulling him closer to her, and he fought against it the only way he knew how. He tried to joke his way out. "Well, don't think I'm going to come over every night and tuck you into bed."

As jokes go, it was a miserable failure. The silence between them was uncomfortable, and he could almost feel her struggling to come up with some suitable reply. Thankfully, Janet picked that moment to end the class and save them.

He helped Whitney to her feet, pulling a little too hard so that she bumped into him once she was standing.

"Sorry," they both muttered.

They didn't talk much on the way home. Doug wanted to say something to lighten the mood, but considering his earlier botched attempt at humor, he decided it was better just to keep quiet.

Finally, after what seemed like the longest drive of his life, he pulled into Whitney's driveway. "Do you need help with anything?"

"No thanks. I'm fine. So, will I see you tomorrow?"

He frowned. "Tomorrow? Do we have another class so soon?"

She laughed and shook her head. "No. Tomorrow's the church Harvest Festival. Remember? Big picnic, games, lots of people? I thought for sure you'd be going."

Doug smacked his forehead with his palm. "Sure, of course I remember the Harvest Festival. I've just been so busy lately, it completely slipped my mind that it's tomorrow. But I definitely want to go. What time should I pick you up?"

"Oh no," she waved her hands in front of him as if trying to flag someone down. "I wasn't wrangling for a lift. I just wanted to know if you'd be there. I'm perfectly capable of driving myself."

Doug smiled. Now they were back on familiar territory. The childbirth class had been a little too close for comfort. But attending a church function and arguing about driving together was something he could handle. "Whitney, there's absolutely no reason we can't carpool. Think of it as doing our part for the environment."

The corner of her mouth lifted in a smirk. She saw right through him, he knew, but she was still going to give in. "Well, if you put it that way, I guess I really can't say no. Should I expect you about eleven?"

"Sounds great."

Whitney gathered up her purse and pillow and got out of the truck. "See you tomorrow!" she called as she walked to her house.

Doug waved and called back, "Lock your door!"

He wasn't sure if it was a laugh or a groan he heard from her as the door closed behind her.

★ ★ ★ ★ ★

Whitney still didn't know what belonged in that picture.

"Something's missing. What do you think, Cliff?"

He stood close behind her, his arms wrapped around her thick waist and his chin resting on her shoulder. "I don't know. I guess you're going to have to figure it out for yourself."

She turned in his arms and looked directly into his eyes. "What do you mean?"

He cradled her face in his palms and kissed her gently, almost reverently. "I've got to go. Good-bye, Whitney." Then he turned and walked out of her studio.

"Cliff?"

She followed him through the hall and into the living room, all the while calling his name. "Cliff!" But he never turned around. He just walked out the front door and closed it behind him. She didn't even get to say good-bye.

Then there was a knock. He hadn't left her after all! She ran to the door and yanked it open. But it wasn't Cliff who stood outside. It was Doug.

"Good morning, Whit."

She just stared at him, not saying a word. He walked to her, put his hand on her shoulder, and started to shake her gently. "Whitney . . . hey, Whit, . . . wake up."

Her eyes flew open and she found herself face to face with Doug, who was crouched by the side of her bed, grinning.

"What are you doing here?" Her mouth was dry and her voice came out in a croak.

He shook his finger at her. "You left your door unlocked again. I thought I'd come over and help you get ready for the Harvest Festival."

She rubbed her eyes and sighed. It had just been a dream. She'd had a lot of dreams about Cliff right after the accident. Dreams where he came back and said everything was all right and they'd be together forever. But never one like this. Never one where he'd said good-bye.

She looked back at Doug and realized he must have said something to her, because he was waiting for an answer. "I'm sorry. What did you say?"

"Do you still feel up to going today?"

He was starting to look concerned, and Whitney knew if she didn't perk up soon, he'd be threatening to drive her to the hospital. "Yeah, of course. I feel fine. Just let me get changed, okay?"

He stood up and nodded. "I'll go wait for you in the front room."

After he'd left the bedroom, Whitney sat up and groaned as she caught a glimpse of herself in the dresser mirror across the room. What a sight she was! Her face was blotchy, her eyes were red and puffy, her hair was falling every which way, and her clothes were a rumpled mess. *Get a move on girl,* she prodded herself.

Once in the bathroom, she tried to think of how she'd fallen into such a deep sleep so fast. She'd only meant to lie down for a few minutes, but she'd slept for over an hour. Of course, that was probably because she'd had so little sleep last night.

Last night. It had been such a roller coaster.

During the film, she'd been caught up in the miracle of birth. It was so incredible to think there was a little person growing inside her, and in just a few short months that person would greet the world. But when the lights went on in the room and the exercises started, all she could think of was how close Doug was and how good it felt to be able to lean against him.

But when he'd joked about tucking her in at night, she'd been ashamed of herself. Not because of the suggestion, but because when he'd said it, her first thought was that she wished he could. Just thinking of it now made her cheeks flush hot.

She turned on the faucet in the basin and splashed cool water on her face. What was she thinking? Cliff had been gone for only five months, and she was getting moony over his brother! It was wrong on so many different levels.

Not anymore, she thought as she buttoned her shirt. This was going to end today!

"God, be with me," she prayed, running the brush through her hair a little too vigorously. "Keep my raging hormones in line and help me remember that Doug is off limits."

The bedroom door opened.

"I'm ready," Whitney announced.

Doug looked up from the magazine he'd been paging through and was amazed at what he saw. She was loaded. She had her camera slung over one shoulder, the camera bag over the other, a big canvas bag dangling from the crook of her elbow, two webbed folding chairs swinging from the other arm, and she somehow managed to drag a heavy Indian blanket behind her.

Doug jumped to his feet. "Are you crazy? Drop that stuff!"

No sooner were the words out of his mouth than Whitney stopped dead in her tracks and dropped all of it, with the exception of her camera, on the floor. They stared blankly at each other for a moment and then burst into laughter.

She looked beautiful. There was nothing spectacular about what she'd done to get ready. She wore jeans and a long-sleeved, white button-down maternity shirt. Her hair was pulled back into a simple ponytail held with a big clip at the base of her neck. But as she laughed, her green eyes sparkled, and her smile was so honestly joyful that there was no other way to describe her. She took his breath away.

And he was staring at her.

Not knowing what else to do, he began picking up the items she'd dropped, and said the first thing that came to his mind.

"Woman, I don't understand you! There you stand, looking like you swallowed a beach ball, and you're trying to carry the whole house outside! I'm going to put this in the truck, and I'll be right back."

Doug picked everything up off the floor and took it outside. Once it was safely stowed in the back of his pickup, he went back into the house. Now Whitney was sitting quietly on the couch. She wasn't smiling anymore, but at least she wasn't trying to carry half of her belongings outside.

"Now that's more like it," he said. "Is there anything else you want to take?"

She motioned halfheartedly toward the kitchen. "There's a big jug of lemonade in the fridge. But I've still got to put together some sandwiches."

Doug nodded. "You just sit there and I'll take care of it."

His tone was so authoritative it made her bristle. She might look like a beached whale, but that certainly didn't mean she was helpless!

"You don't need to do that," she said, launching herself from the couch and sailing past him into the kitchen. "I could make sandwiches before you came home, and I'm perfectly capable of making them now."

Doug followed her, careful to keep out of her way. Something was stuck in her craw, but he had no idea what it was. He stood back and watched her yank open the refrigerator door, rummage through the various drawers, and toss the sandwich fixings on the counter. The way she was throwing things around made him feel sorry for the cold cuts.

"Can I at least give you a hand?" he asked carefully.

She didn't say a word, but pushed the loaf of bread toward him. This was going to be a long day if he couldn't find a way to bring her out of her funk. "How many of these are we going to make?"

"That depends on how hungry you are," she snapped.

He rubbed his chin thoughtfully. "Hmm. Okay, three for me."

"Three?" Her eyebrows shot up in amazement. "You know, there's going to be a lot of other food at the picnic. All kinds of salads, appetizers, desserts . . . are you sure you want three sandwiches?"

He smiled. Obviously he had shocked her out of her mood. "Yes, I definitely want three. And we'll make two for you."

She shook her head. "I only need one."

"Okay, then we'll take an extra for me." She was about to interrupt him, but he hurried on and didn't give her a chance. "So, we've got five sandwiches to make. Perfect."

"Perfect for what?"

He grinned, and said in a conspiratorial whisper, "Perfect for me to share with you one of my hidden talents. Stand back, please."

He pulled a stack of bread out of the package, then dealt the slices out on the counter top as if they were cards. Next, he slapped a layer of mayonnaise on every other slice, dropped the knife in the sink, swiped up the mustard bottle, then deftly squeezed a squiggle of mustard onto the mayonnaiseless slices. He then repeated his card-dealing trick with the sandwich meat and cheese singles. For the big finale, he put the two halves of each sandwich together and wrapped each one up into a tidy aluminum foil package.

"Ta-da!"

Whitney didn't say a word, just looked from him to the stack of sandwiches and then back at him again. For a moment, he was sure that his sandwich-making show had been a big mistake. After all, she'd said she didn't need any help, and then he'd gone and done the whole thing for her. He was getting ready to apologize when her mouth lifted in a grudging smile.

"Bravo," she said, slowly clapping her hands. "Where did you ever learn to do that?"

"Back when all us kids were in school, Mom used to have me fix lunch for everybody. I got pretty good at finding the short-cuts."

"I had no idea you could do that." Whitney pulled an insulated food carrier out of the cupboard and started putting the sandwiches inside. "I'm amazed you never shared your skill with me before now."

He shrugged, then turned to the sink to wash his hands. "Well, it's not exactly a macho-jock kind of skill. At least I didn't think so when I was a teenager."

"And now?"

He turned off the water and shook his hands in the sink, sending droplets flying. "Now, at least it seems to have come in handy."

"In my opinion, there's nothing quite as macho as giving a woman a hand." As soon as the words were out of her mouth, Whitney realized that she'd been upset with Doug moments before just because he offered to help her. Forgive me Lord, she prayed silently, for being so irrational lately. She pulled a hand towel from its hook on the side of the fridge and held it out to him.

Doug reached for the towel at the same moment. He ended up with a handful of cotton, and three of Whitney's fingers. For an instant, neither of them moved. Then Whitney, her cheeks flushed, glanced at the clock on the wall.

"I think we'd better go," she stammered.

Doug nodded his agreement and somehow they made it out to the truck and on their way to the Harvest Festival.

CHAPTER 10

Driving onto the grounds of the Sutter place was like stepping back in time. For as long as anyone could remember it had been the location of the church's annual Harvest Festival. Hyram Sutter had handed the operation, a working Christmas tree farm, down to his sons, but remained an active partner. Known to be quite a character, the old gentleman had always insisted on everyone calling him "Grandpa Hy," even those who weren't that much younger than he.

Doug eased the pickup into an open spot in the designated parking area, then went around to Whitney's side to open the door.

"Why don't we find the rest of the family, and then I'll come back for all of the stuff?"

She nodded and they headed off toward the crowd. The place was already full of people. Children were lined up for the hay maze as well as several carnival style games. In the distance a group of teenagers was playing an impromptu game of touch football. Near a line of tall fir trees, long tables had been set up to hold all the food that people were bringing in. The dessert table alone looked like there wasn't room for one more item.

"Hey," Doug said, still looking at the table, "does Mrs. Swanson still bring her homemade cherry turnovers? Makes my mouth water just thinking about them."

Whitney opened her mouth to answer him, but instead a sharp gasp came out when she stumbled on a rough patch of ground. She needn't have worried. Instinctively, Doug put his hand on her elbow to steady her. She gave him a grateful smile, and she was glad that he left his hand there. For safety's sake, of course.

"Well, there you two are!" Myra Poulten greeted them with hearty enthusiasm. "I was starting to wonder if Doug forgot how to get here. What took you so long?"

Whitney gave Doug a sideways glance, then answered, "We had to throw some sandwiches together."

"They're back in the truck," Doug added with a jerk of his thumb. "I wanted to find you all before we unloaded." He pointed to an empty spot on the big horse blanket that his parents had spread out on the ground. "Whitney, why don't you pull up a corner here, and I'll go get everything."

She took a step forward, then stopped, looking back at him awkwardly. "I don't think . . . I mean, I'm not sure how . . ."

She didn't need to utter another word. He stepped forward, took her hand in his, slipped his other arm around her waist, and helped her lower her very pregnant body gently onto the blanket. Whitney felt the blush creep into her cheeks. What must his family think? But a quick glance in their direction proved they were far more interested in emptying their two large picnic baskets than in anything she and Doug were doing.

Doug crouched beside her. "You going to be okay here till I get back?"

There was something about his nearness and the hand that still held hers that left her speechless. She just nodded.

A piece of hair had escaped her ponytail and fell into her face. He brushed it away, tucking it behind her ear. The look in his eyes was so warm, so deep, that she couldn't look away. She was drowning. Then he ran the back of a finger gently across her cheek. "I'll be back in a second." And with that, he was back up and heading for the pickup.

Whitney watched him go, more than a little shaken by the effect the exchange had on her. And if the huskiness she'd heard in his voice was any indication, he'd felt it too.

Breathe deeply . . . one . . . two . . . three . . .

Doug practiced the breathing they'd learned at the childbirth class. If it could calm a woman in labor, then it surely should help him get his emotions in check.

And it worked. By the time he reached the pickup, his head was clear, and he knew exactly why he had reacted to Whitney that way. He was falling in love with her. The realization didn't make him feel any better.

"Why, Lord?" he muttered to himself as he unloaded the cooler, the blanket, and all the other picnic essentials from the bed of the truck. "Why my brother's widow? Why my sister-in-law? My pregnant sister-in-law? Why couldn't I fall for some simple, unattached female who has no connection to my family?"

He slammed the tailgate shut and started back to the picnic area. Why had he fallen for her? It could simply be a case of supply and demand, he reasoned. After all, he was getting to the age where his family instincts had finally started to kick in. He'd been feeling the need to be rooted, to repair rifts with his family . . . naturally, a wife and children would be part of the picture eventually. And there was Whitney, a ready-made wife and mother all in one package. Other than his mother and sisters, she was the only woman he'd been around much lately, and helping her prepare for the birth of her child had naturally formed a strong bond between them. Sure, that was it. He just needed to get out more, meet other women, and then he'd find someone more suitable for him.

But when he reached the spot where she sat on his parents' blanket, laughing wholeheartedly at one of Hank Poulten's bad jokes, he knew he was done for. He didn't want to get out anywhere or meet any other women. God help him, this was the woman he wanted to be with.

As if sensing him, Whitney turned, still laughing, her smile wide and bright.

"What's so funny?" he asked as he set down the load.

"Your dad told me the joke about the blond girl and the two horses. Have you heard it?"

Smiling, he nodded. "Oh yeah, I'm sure I have." One of Doug's earliest childhood memories was of his father telling blond jokes. This was particularly funny because every one of Hank's children had blond hair of one shade or another. Coming from someone else, the jokes might have seemed insulting, but coming from Hank, they were more like expressions of love.

After Doug spread out their blanket, Whitney scooted over and patted the spot beside her. "Why don't you have a seat? You look a little flushed from all that carrying."

It's not the carrying that's got me flushed, he thought. "I've still got one more trip to make." At her puzzled expression, he added, "I didn't want to drop your camera, so I left it in the truck. Besides, I'd like to say hello to Grandpa Hy."

"Oh, so would I." She wrinkled her nose as she looked up at him. "If you don't mind helping me again, I'll go with you."

"No problem." With a smile he reached out and pulled her to her feet. He felt it again, that warmth when their hands touched. That rightness when she stood next to him.

Trying to distract himself, he looked around. "Where is Grandpa Hy, anyway?"

She looked toward the house. "Probably sitting on the porch."

Doug's brows lifted in amazement. "On the porch? He always used to be right in the middle of everything. I can't imagine him just sitting back and watching."

There was a hint of sadness in Whitney's voice when she

answered him. "Things change, Doug."

And they had changed. When they reached the big farmhouse, Doug saw that the man he'd always thought of as a spry old dog was now sitting placidly in a rocking chair, an afghan draped over his legs, content merely to watch the festivities. He looked thinner than Doug remembered, his face more lined and weathered than it had been, and what little hair he had left stuck up from his scalp in snowy white tufts. It struck Doug that Grandpa Hy must be in his nineties, and again the reality of time marching on without him hit Doug full force.

When he'd decided to come home, the scenario in his mind had been much different from the reality. He'd pictured himself returning to his family's loving embrace. He'd played out in his mind the conversation he and Cliff would have. How they'd mend fences and renew the close friendship they'd once shared. He'd pick up with his old friends and neighbors as if he'd never been gone.

But time hadn't stood still, waiting for him to get his life in order. The folks back home hadn't put their lives on hold until he rejoined them. No, Grandpa Hy had become an elderly man. Some of his old friends had moved away, and those who were still around had families and friends of their own to be concerned with. As for his reunion with Cliff, there hadn't even been a chance to say good-bye.

He glanced over at Whitney, and she smiled gently, as if she knew exactly what he was feeling. But she couldn't know everything. She couldn't know that his anguish wasn't just over the missed time with Cliff, but that he was now betraying his brother in the worst way imaginable, by falling in love with his brother's wife.

She put her hand lightly on his elbow, just enough to get his attention. "Why don't we go on up?"

He nodded and they went up the porch stairs. When they

were standing in front of the old gentleman, Whitney smiled brightly and took his frail hand in hers. "Good morning, Grandpa Hy."

Grandpa Hy looked up at her, then at Doug, then back at Whitney. He blinked his watery blue eyes a few times, and then smiled with recognition. "Oh, if it's not the young Poulten couple. It's so good to see you. When's that youngster of yours coming?"

It took Doug a moment to comprehend what had happened. *He thinks I'm Cliff,* Doug finally realized. He looked at Whitney, and though she hadn't changed positions, her face was ashen and her smile had become stiff, as though frozen in place.

Just then, Grandpa Hy's daughter, Helen, came over from the nearby porch swing she'd been sitting on. "Daddy," she said gently, "This is Doug Poulten. Do you remember him?"

"Doug?" His brow creased as he tried to place the name. Then he began to nod slowly. "Oh yes, Doug. He's the oldest Poulten boy. He moved away quite a while ago. Just up and left with nary a word to anyone. Have you heard from your brother lately, Cliff?"

Doug felt himself pale. "No sir, I haven't." It was useless to try and convince the man he was anyone else. The best thing he could do was remove Whitney from the situation as soon as possible. "If you'll excuse us, sir, we'd better go get some lunch."

Grandpa Hy nodded knowingly. "Yesiree, you'd best make sure that wife of yours doesn't go hungry." He looked up at Whitney, completely guileless and innocent. "After all, you're eating for two now."

Helen looked anxiously at them, as if asking forgiveness for her father's ramblings. Whitney just shook her head slightly, signaling there was no need for Helen to be concerned, then gave Grandpa Hy's hand a gentle squeeze. "You're absolutely right. It was so good seeing you again."

As they turned to walk away, Doug slipped his arm around Whitney's waist. "You're shaking," he said in concern. "Are you okay?"

She nodded and answered a little too quickly. "I'm fine. Let's just get my camera and have some fun, shall we?"

"Okay." He kept his arm around her as they walked, not at all convinced that everything was all right.

Once at Doug's truck, Whitney sat down in the passenger seat and made a production out of going through her camera bag. Then she looked up at Doug, who stood with his arm slung over the open cab door.

"Why don't you go on back? I'll be there in a minute."

He looked uncertain, and for a moment she thought he was going to insist on waiting for her. But then he took a step back and put his hands in the pockets of his jeans. "Okay, if you're sure you're all right."

She flashed him a grin. "I'm great. I'll be there in a few minutes."

He walked away, and as soon as he was out of sight she let the plastic grin fall away from her face. She stared down at her camera, no longer fiddling, but lost in her own thoughts.

The conversation with Grandpa Hy had upset her more than she wanted to admit. Not because he'd thought Doug was Cliff, though. Grandpa Hy had started confusing a lot of people, and there was enough of a family resemblance between the two brothers to understand how he could have gotten mixed up. The awful thing was, it had brought back all the guilty feelings she'd been having.

Whitney took in a deep breath, then let it out slowly. Like childbirth class. A small smile lifted the corners of her mouth as she remembered the look on Doug's face as they'd watched the birthing film. He'd been positively green. She thought of the exercises they'd done together, and how safe and protected he made her feel.

She shook her head sharply, as if to banish the images and the feelings from her head. What's going on, Lord? Her silent prayer just filled her with more questions. Why was she so drawn to Doug, of all people? Not that he wasn't attractive . . . any single woman in the county would give her eyeteeth to go out with him. And he was warm, and he made her laugh, and he had that endearing little habit of rambling whenever he was nervous.

But he was Cliff's brother. That one fact nullified everything else. It didn't matter how right it felt to be with him, or how much she thought of him. It had to stop. Period.

"Help me, Lord," she whispered. "Help me figure out what to do."

"That camera must be giving you a heap of trouble if you're praying over it."

Whitney looked up quickly at the sound of the female voice. She was shocked to see Shawna Williams standing in the same place that Doug had been a few moments earlier. Of all the people that could show up today, this was the last person Whitney had expected to see.

Like Doug, Shawna had been desperate to escape the small town she'd been brought up in. Unlike Doug, she'd never been courageous enough to set out on her own to make it happen. Instead she'd decided the best way out was to marry someone who would take her away. But three divorces later, Shawna still hadn't found her deliverer.

Whitney was amazed that Shawna had come to the Harvest Festival. Shawna wasn't exactly a churchgoer, and she definitely wasn't one to attend church-sponsored functions. Particularly ones that were held outside where she might get dirty or break a nail.

"Shawna." Whitney chose to ignore the woman's earlier

remark. "What a surprise to see you."

Shawna waved her hand carelessly, and Whitney caught a glimpse of bright red, meticulously manicured nails. "I know. I usually don't come to these church picnics . . . not quite my speed. But a little birdie told me this one might be interesting."

"Well, I'm glad to see you." For the life of her, Whitney couldn't figure out what had caught Shawna's interest. Other than the puppet show that was planned for the children, all the other events were the same that took place every year at the Harvest Festival. But Shawna scanned the crowd until she found what she was looking for.

"Yes, sir," she chirped, "it looks like that birdie was right."

Whitney followed her gaze, and then it all made sense. Shawna was staring, practically drooling, at Doug. Whitney's stomach jerked as select images paraded through her head: Doug and Shawna together. The two of them at the Sadie Hawkins Dance, pressed a little too close and moving not nearly enough during a slow dance. Doug, the popular quarterback, and Shawna, the head cheerleader, in their own private huddle after a football game. Whitney forced a smile to her face as she pulled herself back to the present moment. What had brought that on? And why did old high school memories make her feel so uneasy?

"Oh yeah," Whitney said with a nod. "Doug's back."

Shawna grinned. "I see. So, what's he up to these days?"

Whitney felt a bit uncomfortable talking to Shawna about Doug. True, they had been an item once, but that was a long time ago, and Doug had changed a lot. Shawna, on the other hand, hadn't changed much at all. Doug might not want to have the first thing to do with Shawna, especially in light of what he'd confided about their break up.

But then again, Whitney had no way of knowing that. With chagrin, she realized that a spark of jealousy had been kindled at the very thought of Doug and Shawna even talking to each other. Well, maybe that was just what Doug needed. It most certainly was what Whitney needed . . .—a reality check. Doug was an attractive, single man and there was no reason he shouldn't have a conversation with an attractive, single, albeit shallow, woman.

Whitney shrugged and looked up at Shawna. "You know, I think he'd probably like to catch up with you himself. Why don't you go talk to him?"

She caught a glimmer of surprise in Shawna's eyes, as though she'd expected Whitney to object, but just as quickly it was gone. Her full, pouty lips pulled back in a smile to reveal the most perfect teeth Whitney had ever seen. "I like how you think. I'll see you later."

With that, she flounced off. Whitney watched as Shawna walked up to Doug. She caught the surprise on Doug's face when he turned around to see Shawna standing there. And although Shawna reached out first, Whitney couldn't help but notice that Doug hugged her right back without any resistance.

There they stood. Shawna, with her perfect teeth, blond hair just so, looking trim in her designer jeans and turtleneck, and Doug, handsome as ever, his rugged charm the ideal contrast to Shawna's petite beauty. They looked perfect together, just like they always had.

That nauseous feeling came back, but Whitney couldn't attribute it to simple hunger or morning sickness. What had she done?

CHAPTER 11

Quite a few eyebrows had risen when Doug Poulten volunteered to be the anchorman for the red team during the traditional tug-of-war. Nobody was as surprised, however, as Doug himself.

He'd had no choice, really. It had been the only way to distance himself from Shawna.

He'd been more than a little rattled to see her at the picnic, and even more so when she hugged him hello. This was one blast from his past that he didn't welcome. But he'd been polite. He'd hugged her back and had made conversation. Unfortunately, she must have misread his intentions, because she'd stuck to him like a bur in a saddle blanket for the next few hours. When he said he needed to meet up with his family, she'd invited herself along. When Pastor Rogers blessed the food, everyone was invited to take the hands of those closest to them. Of course, since Shawna was right next to Doug at the time, he'd had no choice but to take her hand in his. Ironically, Whitney was on his other side, and he found himself holding the hands of two very different women.

It had been humorous to watch Shawna pick her way through the food line. While Doug and Whitney filled their plates with homemade delicacies like fried zucchini, fluffy white biscuits, and sugary donuts, Shawna's plate held a few spoonfuls of salad and some fruit.

Doug couldn't resist needling her just a little. He held up a big, cheesy potato skin and waggled it in front of her. "You're not going to pass up all this good food, are you?"

She made a face. "Do you have any idea how much fat is in that?"

"Can't say that I do." And he really didn't care. He couldn't help but think that Shawna would be a lot happier if she worried less about calories.

Finally, after all the food was eaten and it was time for the games to begin, Doug had seen his way out. Knowing that Shawna had a problem with dirt, he'd volunteered for the tug-of-war.

"Do you want to come over?" he'd asked pleasantly, praying that his instincts had been right.

As he'd hoped she would, she shook her head. "No, thanks," she said, wrinkling her nose in disgust. "There's just too much mud in that pit to suit me."

But Whitney, who had been uncharacteristically quiet for the last few hours, called to him before he could get away. "I want to come with you."

"Really?" He turned to her, trying not to let his pleasure show.

"Sure. This is too good a photo-op to miss. And you know me and mud. We're like this." She held up two crossed fingers, reminding him of that first day he'd been home and their encounter in the mud puddle. "But as you also know," she continued, "I need a crane or something to help me up. Do you mind?"

She held out her hand to him, and he gently eased her to her feet. He turned just in time to see Shawna glaring at them before she turned and walked off in a huff. Just as well, he thought. He wasn't trying to hurt Shawna's feelings, but he didn't want to mislead her either. Shawna might want to fan the flames of their old romance, but as far as he was concerned, those embers were cold and dead.

Now, as Doug took his place at the rope in front of his team-mates, he was keenly aware of every eye on him. It was unlike him, he knew, to volunteer for something as unglamorous and unflattering as this, but then, a lot had changed in the past few years.

He searched the crowd for Whitney and found her immediately. She was already looking through her camera, intent on framing the shot to come. He groaned inwardly and shook his head. Wonderful. Not only was he about to be publicly humiliated, but it would be recorded on film for all time.

As if reading his thoughts, Whitney lowered her camera and gave him a thumbs-up. "Do us proud, Poulten!" she called.

"You got it, Poulten!" he called back. He saw her move her camera back into ready position and was just about to say something else to her when the whistle blew, indicating the beginning of the event. Caught off guard, Doug felt the rope tighten with a jerk, pulling him off balance, and he was unceremoniously thrown into the midst of the mud pit.

The crowd erupted with gasps and laughter. Even the opposing team was laughing so hard that they couldn't pull on the rope. The red team, however, saw this as their chance for victory and put all their muscle behind them. When John Gillis, the anchor for the blue team, realized what was happening, he became suddenly serious.

"Put your backs into it, men!" he yelled, rallying his team, and the war was on.

Doug got to his feet and moved back to his place at the front of his team. He was covered in brown, cold, oozing mud. What he really wanted to do was find a hot shower, but his team was struggling. For some reason, even though it was just a silly picnic game with no real meaning behind it other than fun, the tug-of-war suddenly became very important to Doug, as though finishing, and possibly winning, would give him back some of what he'd lost during the time he'd been away from his friends and family.

He took hold of the rope and realized at once that his hands were too muddy to get a good grip. He tried wiping them off on his blue jeans, but that was an exercise in futility. Frustration welled up inside him. Maybe he'd be better off quitting after all. But then, out of the corner of his eye, he noticed something white flapping beside him. He turned and saw Whitney, standing far enough away to stay out of the mess, but close enough for him to reach out and grab the handkerchief she was waving at him. He was glad to see it was a big man's handkerchief, definitely big enough to be useful.

She smiled at him when he took it. He quickly wiped off his hands and face, then tossed it to the side. "Thanks, Whit."

She didn't say anything in return. Just winked at him, took a few steps back, and put her camera to her face again. Back to her job as unofficial Harvest Festival photographer.

Doug grabbed the rope and pulled with all his might. Behind him, he heard a cheer go up from his teammates. One fellow called out, "Now we're gonna win this thing!" And in a brief flash, when Doug looked up at John Gillis, who was mirroring him on the other side of the mud pit, the man gave him a quick nod of approval.

Despite the chill in the air, compounded by the cold mud soaking through his clothes, Doug felt warmed. Warmed by the support of his friends, by the feeling of being part of a group effort, no matter how trivial the effort was. But mostly he felt warmed to the core of his soul by Whitney's thoughtful gift of the handkerchief and her wink of encouragement. That one small gesture, more than anything else, communicated volumes. He felt included, special, wanted. He felt loved.

One of the wonderful things about being a photographer and

artist was that no one thought twice when Whitney was taking pictures. If they'd seen her merely staring intently at Doug, surely people would have talked. But instead, looking through her viewfinder, she was ignored.

So she kept taking pictures.

No one was aware that, through the use of her zoom lens, she was focusing exclusively on Doug rather than the entire game. It was Doug who filled the frame. His body tensing as he pulled on the rope, his hands gripping it as though it were a lifeline. She zoomed in even tighter, and now Doug's face was sharp and clear. The muscles in his neck stood out like steel cords and his jaw was firmly set. Despite the coolness of the day, tiny beads of sweat had formed on his forehead. He was taking this more seriously than most people would. Whitney certainly hadn't expected it to mean so much to him.

And then a look passed over his face. It was as though something had just come to him, some thought that made him . . . what? Content? Yes, if she had to put a name on it, she'd say he looked content and happy to be exactly where he was. She hadn't sensed that feeling in him for quite some time. In fact, the entire time he'd been home she'd been waiting to see if he would really stay. A part of her kept expecting him to become restless again and need to move on. But now, seeing that look on his face, no matter how fleeting it was, made her smile.

A shout went up from the crowd around her. Finally, she dropped her camera and took in what was going on. They were winning! The red team was doing it!

She had time for only one more quick picture—of the flag crossing over to the red team's side—and it was over. Then she joined the rest of the crowd as they applauded for everyone who had participated in the game.

Whitney watched as the red and blue teams mingled,

congratulating or good-heartedly consoling each other. Then Doug broke free from the group and sauntered her way.

He held both his arms straight out from his sides. "I guess this mud bath thing runs in the family."

She laughed, shaking her head. "I guess it does." Then a gust of wind hit her and she grew serious. He must be freezing. "You probably want to go home and change, huh?"

"No way," he replied adamantly. "A Poulten never wins and runs. I've got a change of clothes in the truck."

"Were you expecting this to happen?"

"No, but working with horses has gotten me into the habit of always being prepared. I can't tell you how many times I've looked just like this."

She laughed and wiggled one eyebrow at him. "Oh, so this isn't the first time you've landed face down in the mud?"

"Far from it." He dipped his head and finished with a thick cowboy accent. "Why, little lady, I could tell you stories that would make your head swim."

"I'm sure." She looked around and realized there was only one place where he could change. "You're going to have to go into the house, but," she added, looking him up and down, "you can't possibly go inside like that. You'd make a huge mess."

"I hadn't thought about that, but you're right." He frowned, thinking. Then he snapped his fingers. "I've got it. I'll just go to the creek and wash off the worst of the mud. If I remember right, there's a bathroom just inside the back door of the house. At least that way, I'll just drip water on the floor. That'll be easy to clean up before I leave."

Just then Sarah ran up carrying one of the horse blankets they'd been sitting on while they ate. "Good job, bro. I didn't know you had it in you."

"You're not the only one," he returned with a smirk. "Is that for me?"

"Yeah, I thought you might want to wrap up with something."

"Thanks, kiddo. Hey, do me a favor." He dug in his pocket, pulled out his slightly muddy key ring and tossed it to her. "There's a black duffel bag behind the passenger seat of my truck. Would you get it for me? Just leave it by the back door of the house. I'm going to the creek to wash off."

"Sure." She started to hand him the blanket but thought better of it. "On second thought, maybe you'd better take this, Whitney. You're a whole lot cleaner."

Whitney laughed as Sarah dodged the playful swat Doug took at her as she jogged off toward his truck.

Now that Whitney was holding the blanket, she had no choice but to stay with Doug. Neither said anything as they made their way to the creek. When they got there, Doug pulled off his boots and socks. Then he took off his shirt and threw it to the side. "No sense getting completely soaked," he said to Whitney with a smile, and he waded into the creek, jeans and all.

Whitney watched as the coldness of the water hit him. He took in a great gasp of air and his abdominal muscles contracted, becoming rock hard. His jaws were visibly clenched, but she knew he didn't want her to see that the cold bothered him. "How's the water?" she asked sweetly.

"Great," he boomed. "Just great. Care to join me?"

Whitney knew better. Even in the height of summer the creek was pretty chilly. In mid-October, they were lucky it hadn't started to ice over yet. "Oh no. One cold, freezing wet Poulten at a time is quite enough."

He knelt down and bent over, putting is face briefly into the water then throwing his head back with a shout. Droplets of water flew from his hair and he swiped one hand across his wet face.

"Exhilarating!" He called out to Whitney as he stood up. She was sure he was understating the obvious. From the way his skin was turning bright red, she could tell just how frigid the water really was.

Next he rubbed at his jeans, washing away most of the dirt. As he leaned over, something beneath the surface caught his attention. He scooped it up and walked over to her. "Hey, Whit, look at this!"

She peered at the handful of stones he held out to her. "Hmm. Nice rocks."

"These aren't just any rocks," he said in mock indignation. "These are skipping rocks. Remember?"

And suddenly she did, as if it had just happened. The day that Doug had tried, and failed, to teach her how to skip rocks. It was the first weekend after the start of school and Whitney had still been madly in love with him. She, Doug, and Cliff had been fishing on the other end of the creek on the Poulten property, but nothing was biting. Finally, the two brothers had engaged in a rock-skipping contest. Doug had won, of course, and Whitney had tried to console Cliff.

"I don't know how you do it at all," she'd said. "I've never been able to skip a rock."

That was all Doug needed to hear. Right then, he'd taken it upon himself to teach her. At first he'd just shown her. He told her how to hold the rock, demonstrated the finger positions and then the form. But while his rock danced across the top of the water five times before sinking, hers plummeted to the depths of the creek with a dull plunk.

She remembered how frustrated she'd been. She wanted to impress Doug . . . to do it right because he could do it, and because he was teaching her. But when her third try drilled into the bank of the creek without even hitting the water, she gave up.

"It's no use," she said shaking her head. "I'm never going to get this!"

But Doug wasn't taking no for an answer. "Here, do it this way." He walked right up to her, grabbed her hand and put the rock in it. Then he positioned her fingers. "You don't want to hold the top of it," he said matter of factly. "The trick is to hold it around the edges."

Then, while still holding her hand, he'd stepped behind her. "And this is how you want to swing."

Her heart was beating so hard she was sure he'd be able to feel it, even though he was standing behind her. But as usual, Doug was oblivious to everything going on around him. It was a rock-skipping lesson, nothing more.

He moved her hand in a smooth arc a few times and then stepped away. "Now try it."

Somehow, she'd pulled it together long enough to give the stone a halfhearted throw. It skimmed the water once, then disappeared. Whitney couldn't remember what happened after that, except that it had been the last time she'd ever tried to skip a rock.

Now Doug was grinning at her, dripping wet and holding out the rocks as if in challenge. She knew that, at the time, he'd had no idea how he affected her. But was he aware of it now?

"You know I can't skip rocks worth beans." She made her remark as flip and offhanded as possible, but something in his eyes told her he wasn't buying it.

He waded out of the creek and walked up to her, arm still outstretched. "Come on. I'll show you how. It'll be fun."

It'll be fun? She imagined him standing behind her again, his arm wrapped around her as he demonstrated proper rock-skipping form. To be that close to him right now, to feel him touch her, would not be fun. Just thinking about it made her yearn to give in, to go into his arms and tell him to forget the rocks. She just wanted to be enfolded in his arms. And that was torture, because it was the one thing she could never have.

He took another step. He was close to her now. So close. Too close.

She shook her head sharply. "Forget about it. You're all wet." Her words came out a little too sharply and she could tell he wasn't entirely sure whether she meant he was physically or metaphorically all wet, but that couldn't be helped. Before he could say another word she handed him the blanket. "Here. I'm going back to the picnic. I'll meet you there."

Whitney walked away without another look and he didn't try to stop her. She knew she should be happy. She should be glad that she'd gotten out of the situation relatively unscathed. But she was miserable. The last thing she'd wanted to do was walk away from Doug. But she couldn't have what she wanted. Cliff hadn't been gone long enough for her to be having feelings like this, and worse yet, she was having the feelings for his brother.

No, she told herself. Walking away was the right thing to do. There was no sense in putting herself in situations that made her miserable. But at the same time, she knew she'd left a little piece of her heart back there with Doug.

CHAPTER 12

By the time Doug got himself cleaned up and changed his clothes, the picnic had begun to break up. He was on his way to look for his family when someone walked up behind him and tapped him on the shoulder. He turned quickly, hoping it was Whitney, but instead he saw Shawna smiling at him.

"My goodness, don't you clean up well."

"Thanks." Doug was still uneasy around her. "I'm surprised you haven't taken off already."

Her lips pursed into a pout. There was a time when she could get Doug to do anything she wanted just by making that sad, little girl face. Now it just made Doug feel embarrassed for her.

"And not say good-bye to you? Never. Besides," she added, slipping her arm through his, "I was hoping maybe you and I could ditch this place together."

This is what Doug had been afraid of. For some reason, Shawna had now decided that he was good enough for her and was determined to get him back. And when Shawna wanted something, she didn't let it go without a fight.

"I really can't go anywhere," he answered, hoping to let her down gently. "I brought Whitney, and I need to get her home." From the surprised look on her face, he could tell that Shawna wasn't used to being turned down by men. And the fact that Doug was choosing to stay with a pregnant woman rather than go with her probably stung more than a little. Still, she wasn't about to give up.

"Isn't that sweet of you? But you know, you could drop her off and then come over to my place." She ran her manicured fingernails gently down his arm. "It's been so long since we've spent any time alone together. I'd really love to catch up with you."

The subtle approach obviously wasn't going to work. Gently, Doug removed her hand from his arm. "Shawna, I'm not interested in catching up."

She frowned, accentuating the lines around her mouth that she tried so hard to erase with makeup. "You're not still upset about that little spat we had in high school, are you?"

"Spat?" Doug couldn't keep from laughing. "You broke up with me because I couldn't play football anymore. That was a lot more than a spat."

"I'm sorry about that, Doug." Her mouth softened and her lashes dipped. At that moment, it seemed to Doug that she genuinely was sorry. "It was incredibly shallow of me, I know. I just wanted to get out of this town so bad, and when it looked like you weren't going pro, well . . . I guess I panicked. My goal back then was to be with somebody who had prospects." She smirked, shaking her head. "And look at us now. I ended up still stuck here, and you went and made something of yourself, anyhow. I hurt you for nothing, and believe me, I've regretted it ever since." She reached up and put her hand against his cheek. "You can't have forgotten how good we were together. You and I had something really special. Don't you think we owe it to ourselves to try again?"

Doug pulled her hand from his face and took a good look at Shawna. She tried to be so tough, but he could see the hurt and desperation in her eyes. She thought she needed a romance, that finding the right man would be the answer to all her problems. But what she really needed was a friend.

"It seems to me," he said slowly, "that you've been looking

for a savior for a lot of years. Why don't you come to church with me sometime, and I'll introduce you to mine?"

She gaped at him, eyes wide. She couldn't have looked more shocked if he'd slapped her. "You've got to be kidding. Since when did you find religion?"

"Not religion. Faith," he said with a smile. "And it found me, right in the nick of time. Shawna, I'd like to be your friend, but that's all there can ever be between us."

She was smarting from his rejection, he could tell. But in typical Shawna style, she lashed out rather than admit she was hurt. "Wow, I guess I made the right choice, after all. You're just as pitiful as the rest of these Bible thumping saps."

Doug watched as she walked quickly away. He only hoped she would think about what he'd said and maybe one day take him up on his invitation. Lord, he prayed silently, work in Shawna's heart. Let her discover what true love really is.

Finally Doug found his parents by the tree where they'd eaten lunch. They were cleaning things up, folding blankets and putting empty food containers back in the picnic basket.

"Hey guys, do you need any help?"

His mother looked up with a smile and shook her head. "No, this is the last of it."

Sarah bounced up to him holding a big canvas bag. "Here, this is Whitney's. She forgot to take it with her."

For a moment he felt something close to panic at the realization that Whitney was nowhere to be seen. Had she left with someone else? Was she that upset with him? "Where is Whitney?"

"She decided to wait for you in the truck," his dad answered. "It's been a pretty long day for her. I'd say she's just pure worn out."

Myra looked at him thoughtfully. "You know, her whole mood seemed to change after the tug-of-war. I guess all the excitement just caught up with her. You should probably get her right home."

"That's a good idea." He gave his mother a kiss on the cheek and, with a wave to the rest of the family, set off for the parking area.

He relaxed a little. If she was waiting for him, she couldn't be as mad as he'd thought she was. Knowing Whitney, she'd have taken off on foot rather than let him drive her if she'd been really upset. But as he got closer to his truck, he felt himself tensing again, because Shawna was standing beside the vehicle, talking to Whitney.

Whitney sat in the passenger seat of the pickup, her head throbbing. The encounter with Doug by the creek had been the last straw for her. It was now painfully clear that her emotions were running rampant and she was feeling things for him she had no right to feel. And what about Doug? What was he feeling? He said things that made her think he was attracted to her too. But was he really, or was he just teasing? On one hand, she wanted to know the attraction she saw in his eyes was real. But on the other hand, she knew it would be disastrous if it was. She felt like she was being ripped in half.

She closed her eyes and put her head back against the seat. "Oh God," she whispered, "what am I going to do?"

"My goodness, pregnant people do talk to themselves a lot."

Whitney's eyes flew open and her head jerked around. Once again, Shawna had walked up to her at an inopportune moment. And Whitney was in no mood to play nice.

"And single people eavesdrop a lot," she answered back, sugar sweet.

Shawna tipped her head, her look almost impressed. "Touché. Actually, I saw you sitting over here, and I just wanted to let you know that if you need anything, I'm only a phone call away."

Now Whitney felt guilty. Maybe Shawna had changed since they were in high school. "Thanks, Shawna. That's nice of you."

"I know how hard it must be, with your husband gone and all. I mean, you've really got no one to rely on."

Whitney's stomach lurched. It was probably from too much potato salad. "I'm really doing fine. The Poultens are like my own parents, you know. And Doug's been wonderful."

Shawna smiled, but her eyes were like ice. "Doug is wonderful, isn't he? I think it's so sweet how he's filling in for his little brother. Who knew he had such a sense of duty?"

Whitney's mouth was dry and she was feeling sick. She didn't like where this conversation was going. She wanted to say that duty had nothing to do with Doug's feelings for her, but the words wouldn't come out. It wouldn't have mattered even if they had, because Shawna was still talking.

"I for one am thrilled he's tied to you until you have that baby. That way, I know he'll be around for a while. You know, I wouldn't be surprised if he just picked up and took off again the day after that youngster is born. He never could stand living in this hick town. Why he would come back if he could help it is beyond me."

Shawna's pretty mouth turned down into a sneer, reflecting just how she felt about being in a "hick town." *I wasn't wrong about Shawna,* Whitney thought. *She hasn't changed a bit.*

"So what keeps you here?" Whitney asked.

A shadow of a frown crossed Shawna's face, and for a moment Whitney felt guilty. She knew good and well that if any of Shawna's husbands had kept his word to her, Shawna would be long gone. As tough as she was, Whitney still thought the breakup of three marriages had to hurt.

But Shawna didn't let her feelings show for long. She smirked, cocked her head to the side and put one hand on her hip. She looked like a model striking a pose. "Well, there are some natural attractions in these parts that you just can't find anywhere else. In fact, here comes one now."

With morbid fascination, Whitney watched Shawna saunter over to Doug as he approached the truck. His arms were full and Shawna took advantage of the opportunity. She said something to him, so low that Whitney couldn't make it out, then put her hands on either side of his face, her bright red nails vivid against his sandy hair, and kissed him full on the lips. Whitney told herself not to look. It was none of her business, and it hurt too much . . . but she couldn't stop herself. It seemed as though Shawna and Doug were locked together forever, but in actuality, it took Doug only half a second to extricate himself from Shawna's embrace. He dropped everything he was holding, then grasped her shoulders and pushed her gently away, shaking his head and saying something that Whitney couldn't hear. And then he did the most amazing thing. He looked directly past Shawna and right at Whitney.

As soon as their eyes met, Whitney looked away. She wasn't sure how to read him. Was he sorry she had seen Shawna kiss him? Or was he trying to send her a message? Was he saying, "Look at Shawna and me. How could you possibly think I'd want you, when I could have someone like this?"

In a few minutes, the door on the driver's side opened and Doug got in. Whitney didn't look at him.

"I'm sorry about that," he said.

She kept her gaze steady, looking out the window ahead of her. "No problem."

"Hey." He reached over and covered her hand with his. "Whit? Are you okay?"

She turned to him then. His face was concerned and loving and it just about did her in. But she smiled stiffly and nodded. "I'm okay. Really. It's been a long day, and I'm very tired. I'd just like to go home now."

They stared at each other for a long time. Finally, Doug nodded, started up the truck, and drove toward her home.

It was the longest trip of Whitney's life. She could feel the tension stretched tight between the two of them. She didn't want to think about it, but she couldn't stop her mind from going over what Shawna had said. She'd thought back, from the first day Doug had come home, dissecting every little thing he'd said or done.

He'd told her he wanted to help her through the pregnancy . . . that at least he could do that much for Cliff. He'd spoken to Pastor Rogers about his responsibility to look after a widow. And then, to clinch it, she remembered how he'd told her that very morning that she looked like she'd swallowed a beach ball. It left no doubt in her mind. Shawna was right. He obviously had no personal interest in her at all other than as a responsibility.

The knowledge should make her happy. She should be relieved there were no personal entanglements to worry about. But Whitney felt just the opposite. It was as though a heavy black cloud surrounded her. It was bad enough that she was alone and unattractive. Now Doug felt responsible for her.

No, she wouldn't allow herself to be a burden to anybody. She'd been taking care of herself since she was a teenager. She could take care of this pregnancy on her own too.

The gravel crunched beneath the tires of the truck as Doug pulled into her driveway. When the vehicle stopped, Whitney didn't even look at him. She just got out, shut the door quietly behind her, and went into her house. She didn't even take her camera bag with her.

As soon as she got in the house, Whitney realized her mistake. By leaving everything in the truck, Doug was sure to follow her inside. But she'd just wanted to get away.

The front door opened and Doug came in, again carrying all

of her things. The image cemented her resolve. She decided at that moment it would be the last time he would ever have to carry her load.

"You forgot a few things," he said with a smile.

"I'm sorry. Just put them down anywhere."

He set everything next to the couch, then looked at her, not quite sure what to say. He stuffed his hands in the pockets of his jeans and rocked forward once on the balls of his feet. "So I guess I'll see you Monday. For our next childbirth class."

"No, that's not necessary."

Her words came out more sharply than she'd meant them to. Standing across from her, Doug looked perplexed.

"What do you mean?"

She took a deep breath. Please, Doug, she thought, don't make this any harder on me than it already is. "I mean you don't need to worry about me. I'm fine. You're free to do whatever you like. You're not responsible for me."

"That's it," Doug growled. He crossed the floor and stood in front of her. "You've been mad at me since we left the picnic and I don't know why. You're going to tell me what's going on, and you're going to do it now."

This was the last thing Whitney had expected. Relief, maybe. Noble denial, certainly. But he was downright angry with her. Which made her get angry right back.

"Look, I thought about a lot of things today. I just don't need you hanging around out of a sense of duty. I'm perfectly capable of taking care of things on my own. So go live your happy, carefree life and leave me alone!"

"Duty?" he barked. "Whoever said I was with you out of duty?"

"You did. Remember all that stuff you said about talking to Pastor? You know, the whole 'widows and orphans' thing. Well, I don't need your help, and I don't need you!"

Doug just stood there, his hands on his hips, head down. I nailed him, Whitney thought, and now he's too ashamed to even look at me. Things will never be the same again between us. Even though she knew it was for the best, and it was what she wanted, her heart sank.

But when he finally looked up, she knew she'd been only partially right. Things would never be the same, but not for the reason she thought.

"You are the most exasperating woman I've ever known." His voice was low and controlled, his speech so drawn out that he was practically speaking in one-word sentences. "You completely misread everything I said that day. Now you're passing judgment without any input from me whatsoever. I have half a mind to walk out that door right now and let you fend for yourself."

"Then what's stopping you?" she shot back.

"Because I also love you more than any woman I've ever known."

For a moment, Whitney felt as if the air had been sucked out of the room. But then she came to her senses. He could have meant that only one way.

"Of course you love me. I'm your sister-in-law. But that—"

"No," he cut her off sharply. "I don't love you like a sister. I love you. Whitney, I love everything about you." He moved toward her now, and when he reached up to cup her cheek in his hand, she didn't pull away. "I love the way you chew on your straw when you're drinking a soda. I love how you snort when you laugh really hard. I love how you bite your lower lip when you're concentrating on your work. I love how beautiful and thoughtful you are." Then he smiled the most perfect smile she'd ever seen. "I want to be with you because I've fallen head over heels in love with you."

Whitney's mind was whirling. It briefly occurred to her that she should sit down, but she couldn't make her feet move. All she could do was stare back into Doug's eyes, eyes that were so full of love there was no way for her not to believe what he was saying. She wanted to say it back, tell him how she felt about him, but it just wasn't that easy.

"Doug, I . . . I don't know. What about Cliff?"

His hand fell from her cheek and he stared at the floor again. When he lifted his gaze, she could see the conflict he was going through too. "I know this is hard for you. And it's been hard for me. I've been fighting this since I got back home." He took both of her hands in his and squeezed them. "But Cliff is dead. I know him well enough to believe he wouldn't want you to stop living. Hey, it's not as if we planned this. It's not like we were waiting to be together, right?"

Her thoughts flashed back to the first day of high school. That was so long ago, and yes, it had just been a crush. But she was still ashamed that she had felt any kind of love for Doug before she married Cliff. And this conversation was only making her feel worse.

Before she realized what was happening, she was crying. Were they tears of joy or tears of pain? She was so confused, she couldn't tell the difference. Apparently, neither could Doug, because he pulled her into his arms, hugging her and telling her everything would be all right. "Please, Whitney, don't cry. We'll work this out. I never meant to hurt you, just to love you."

He held her tight and stroked her hair. She remembered the dream she'd had the other night, of Cliff saying good-bye. Is this what it had meant? That she was supposed to let Cliff go and move on? It felt so right to be in Doug's arms, so good to be loved by him. And she was so tired. She just wasn't strong enough to fight anymore.

In her head she thought, I love you too. But the words wouldn't come out. So she held him tighter, hoping that if they stayed there in each other's arms she could ignore everything else.

Still murmuring comforting words, Doug kissed the top of her head. Then his head dipped down and he kissed her cheek. Whitney looked up into his warm, dark eyes, and they froze. For a moment in time, it was just the two of them, alone with their feelings. She knew the kiss was coming before it happened, and she did nothing to stop it. Heaven help her, she didn't want to stop it. The kiss was sweet and gentle, and just about broke Whitney's heart. Her feelings of guilt still danced around the edges of this new and fragile relationship . . . a relationship she couldn't bear to acknowledge as being real.

This was the moment Doug had been waiting for. He had professed his love to Whitney and she was in his arms. He wanted nothing more than to lose himself in the kiss, but he couldn't help being slightly preoccupied. He was afraid that any second she would pull away and begin raving at him again. But in the end, it was Doug who pulled away first, and all because of one well-placed kick.

He felt it against his stomach and immediately jumped back. Pointing down at Whitney's stomach, he asked, "What was that?"

It took her a moment to comprehend why he'd moved from her so quickly, but then the light dawned. "Oh. The baby." Whitney couldn't stop the laughter that bubbled up out of her. "That was the baby kicking."

"Man, he's strong," Doug said in amazement.

Whitney nodded. "Yes, she is."

They were on familiar ground again, bantering about the sex of her unborn child, and it brought a smile to both of them. "That was quite a reaction to a simple kiss," he joked.

The smile on Whitney's face froze in place, and she shook her head. "Believe me, Doug, there was nothing simple about that kiss."

CHAPTER 13

Noah looked like he had a headache.

Whitney frowned and took a step back from the rough draft of the mural she was sketching on the church nursery wall. Her goal had been to make this an image of Noah after the flood. Whereas the usual Noah mural showed the animals tromping into the ark two by two, hers depicted the happy animals fleeing the ark onto dry land. It also showed Noah and his family looking up to God with expressions of praise and thanksgiving. At least, that had been the idea. But her caricaturized version of Noah just seemed to be scowling.

She sat down across the room to get a better overall view of the wall. Maybe Pastor Rogers had been right. He'd told her not to worry about the mural until after the baby came, but that was a whole month away, and Whitney was desperately in need of a project to take her mind off things.

To take her mind off Doug.

Ever since the kissing incident, the mood between them had been strained, to say the least. Thankfully, that night he'd realized that things were going too fast for her. When he left, he'd given her a respectful kiss on the forehead and told her he wasn't going to push.

"I know this is a lot for you," he said. "When you're ready to move forward, let me know."

And then he'd left, locking the door behind him as he always did. Since then, they'd gone to her final childbirth class and had seen each other on Sundays and several other casual occasions, but they never spoke about that night or the feelings that hung between them. Of course that didn't stop Whitney from thinking about all of it.

How could one person be so conflicted? On one hand, she couldn't wait to see him, but those same feelings ate her up with guilt. When she wasn't with him, she thought of him constantly, but when they were together, she felt as if she were doing something wrong. Doug had professed his love for her, but love wasn't supposed to hurt this much.

Heavy footsteps sounded in the hall, bringing an end to her musings. A moment later the tall frame of Pastor Rogers filled the doorway.

"How's our Michelangelo doing?" he asked with a smile.

She pointed to the wall. "You tell me."

He stood in front of her work in progress, looking at it thoughtfully, his hand cupping his chin. "It's good. I like how you've chosen to capture the idea of God fulfilling his promise." He paused for a moment. "Can I ask you one thing?"

"Go ahead."

"At such a happy time, why does Noah look so pained?"

She shook her head. "You're very perceptive. I was just wondering that myself."

Pastor Rogers picked up one of the folding chairs that was leaning against the opposite wall and sat beside Whitney. "Do you think it might possibly be a reflection on the artist?"

She didn't let on that the thought had crossed her mind. Better to hear his take on things without any input from her. "What do you mean?"

"Well, here you are, expecting this baby. That's a blessing, and a fulfillment of a promise from God to you. But at the same time, you've got incredible sorrow because of Cliff's death. Add that to the roller coaster of emotions that go with any pregnancy, and you're dealing with an awful lot."

She looked up at Pastor Rogers. She'd known him practically her whole life. He'd baptized, married, or buried just about everyone in the town. In his kind eyes was reflected the love of the Lord, and she knew beyond a shadow of a doubt that she could trust him. Despite the fact that she tried not to admit her feelings, not even to herself, she knew she needed to talk to someone. Right now, she couldn't think of a better person than the man sitting next to her.

"You're right, Pastor. I've felt all those things. I'm so excited about the baby, but I miss Cliff so much. It kills me to know that my baby will never know her father. But . . ."

She stopped, still hesitant to reveal her true feelings. What would Pastor think when he found out?

"But what?" he asked gently.

"But, that's not all that's bothering me. Pastor, Cliff has only been gone for seven months, and I . . . I . . ." She couldn't force herself to say it. But in the end, she didn't need to.

"You're feeling guilty about Doug."

Whitney was so shocked she actually gasped. Had she been that transparent? "You know? How do you know?"

He smiled. "Anything a member of this congregation says to me in confidence stays that way. But I can let you know that Doug and I have talked on more than one occasion. So why don't you fill me in on your side of things?"

Now that the secret was out, the words poured from Whitney. "Oh, Pastor, it's just so complicated. When Cliff died, I felt like I wanted to die too. I never thought I'd ever fall in love with another man again, and I certainly wasn't looking for someone. But to have it happen this soon . . . and with his brother. It just all seems so wrong."

He smiled and took her hand. "Whitney, every person grieves in a different way. The ability to continue to love, and to love another person, doesn't diminish what you and Cliff shared."

"My head knows that," Whitney replied, "but it's my heart that's having the problem. I just can't stop feeling guilty."

Pastor Rogers thought for a moment, then continued. "Let me ask you this. Did you love Cliff?"

She didn't hesitate with her answer. "Absolutely."

"Were you ever unfaithful to him?"

"No, never!" Whitney was surprised he would even ask such a thing.

Pastor Rogers continued calmly. "Did you ever have desires to be with Doug while you were with Cliff?"

She felt that now-familiar sinking feeling in the pit of her stomach. "No, but . . ."

Now Pastor Rogers frowned. "But what?"

"It's just that, in high school, before Cliff and I got together, I had a crush on Doug. But once I was with Cliff, I never thought about Doug like that again, I swear. Not until now, anyway."

This brought a chuckle out of the pastor. "No wonder you're so confused now. You probably feel like you were lying in wait for the day you and Doug could be together, is that right?"

She nodded, ashamed that he had pinpointed her worst fear.

But the pastor wasn't at all thrown by her admission. "Whitney, a high school crush, no matter how intense it seems at the time, is very different from a mature, loving relationship. I counseled you and Cliff before you were married, and believe me, I've never met a couple more genuinely in love. I know you were both completely committed to each other, but that doesn't mean you can't go on with your life now that Cliff's gone. You've done nothing wrong, in my eyes, in the eyes of the church, or most importantly, in the eyes of God." He put his hands on his knees as if he was about to get up, but then he stopped himself. "One last question. Do you love Doug?"

She hesitated. Did she love Doug? It was a question she'd asked herself more than once. To admit it to herself, in the privacy of her own home, was hard enough. But to say it out loud to another person would make it so definite. There would be no going back. But then, she realized, things never would go back to the way they were, not even if she continued to deny her feelings. Finally she answered his question.

"Yes, I love him."

He patted her hand, got up, and put the chair back. "Then your heart will tell you what to do. And I think it'll help you clear up your problem with old Noah, here."

Back at the Poulten ranch, Doug was trying to keep his mind off his problems in the only way he knew how: hard labor. His father owned a dozen horses, and the arrival of winter meant they spent most of their time in the barn. Which meant that a dozen stalls needed to be mucked out. What better place for Doug to lose himself?

And it would have worked too, if only his father hadn't come to check on him.

"What in heaven's name are you doing?" Hank Poulten boomed as he walked through the door.

Doug turned around and wiped the sweat off his face with the back of his sleeve. "Just cleaning up."

Hank shook his head. "You were shoveling so fast and furious, I thought maybe you'd discovered gold."

"No such luck, Dad. I guess we're going to have to get rich some other way. Which reminds me . . ."

Hank held up his hand, cutting his son off in midsentence. "Don't say another word. Yes, of course I've thought about your business plan. Frankly, son, I'm honored that you'd want to go in with your old man." He smiled then, a sad, almost beaten smile. "It's just that I've been an outfitter my whole life. I don't know if I'm suited for anything else."

Doug leaned the shovel against the stall wall. This was the crux of it, then. To go into business with Doug would mean his father was admitting that a part of his life was over. What Doug needed to show him was that another part of his life would also be beginning. "That's the beauty of it, Dad. You've been around horses forever, and I know you could run this ranch with your eyes closed. I've spent enough time around the business end of it to take over that part. Between the two of us, we can make this a real going concern."

Hank mulled it over, as if reading through a mental checklist. "But what about cash? It's going to take a good chunk of it to start things up. We can't just ride up into the high country and round up the kind of good bloodstock you're talking about raising."

Doug grinned. "I'll be the first to admit, I made plenty of mistakes when I was out on the racing circuit. But one thing I did do was invest wisely. I've got a sizeable piece of seed money tucked away. And I've already contacted some of the people I worked with during my track days. You know, rich folks are always looking for a good tax shelter. A couple of them are very interested about investing in our business." He peeled off his work gloves and extended a clean hand to his father. "So, what do you say?"

Hank removed his hat, scratched his head, and looked up at the ceiling. Then he grinned, and grabbed Doug's hand. "I'd say you've got yourself a partner."

Doug was so happy, the handshake didn't suffice. He pulled his father into him and gave him a bear hug. "Great," he said, pounding him heartily on the back. "That's just great." He couldn't help but think that if only things would work out between him and Whitney, everything would be perfect.

The two men broke from their embrace, and then stood in

an awkward silence. Finally Doug thought of something to say. "Oh, by the way, I spoke to a man in Whitefish who has some really nice quarter horses. One of his mares is in foal, so I'm going to go down and take a look this afternoon. Want to come?"

Hank shook his head. "Sorry, but I can't. Your mother's got me reserved for the day. Have to help her get ready for Thanksgiving."

Doug's eyebrows rose. "Thanksgiving? Already?"

"Well," Hank responded incredulously, giving a dead-on impression of his wife, "it's only a week away, and there's still so much to do!"

The two men laughed, and then Hank thought of a solution. "Say, why don't you take Whitney? She's always looking for something new to take pictures of, and it'd do her good to get out for a bit."

Without knowing it, Hank had hit on the perfect nonthreatening way for Doug to approach Whitney. "Thanks, Dad," he answered. "I think it would do both of us a lot of good."

Whitney had been surprised when Doug invited her to the B&B Ranch, but she knew he'd been even more surprised when she'd agreed to accompany him without an argument. They rode silently in his pickup now, having used up all the safe subjects to talk about, things like how mild the winter had been so far, how the roads weren't usually this clear, and that all the old-timers said it meant the mother of all storms would hit before the year was up. She almost brought up her work on the mural, but decided against it. She was afraid if he knew she'd seen Pastor Rogers he might also guess what they'd talked about, and she didn't want to bring up that subject again. So now, she just sat, wanting to say a lot of things, but not trusting herself with any of them.

It was Doug who finally broke the silence.

"Did I tell you my Dad and I talked again about going into business?"

She shook her head. "No, you didn't, but I figured our visit to a quarter-horse ranch might have something to do with it. Does this mean he said yes?"

"Yep, he said yes." A smile spread across Doug's face.

It was the first completely genuine smile she'd seen from him in quite some time, and it made her just as happy as his news did. "That's absolutely wonderful, Doug."

They went around a bend in the road that was followed by a sharp left that took them straight into the B&B Ranch. A large, hand-carved wooden sign proclaiming the name arched over the long driveway, which was flanked on both sides by white rail fencing. In the distance, they could see several paddocks, what looked like a training arena, and two long barns.

"The place looks nice," Whitney said.

Doug nodded. "You can tell a lot about people from the way they keep up their facility. Only do business with people who treat their horses right, and you can't go wrong."

The pickup's tires crunched on the snow-frosted gravel as Doug parked in front of the first barn. They'd barely had time to leave the vehicle when a stocky man wearing a Stetson and a heavy, fleece-lined suede jacket ran out to meet them.

"I was hoping you'd get here soon," the man called. "Come on!" He ran back into the barn, motioning urgently for them to follow him.

"Who's that?" Whitney asked as they walked quickly inside.

"Bob Henderson," Doug answered. "He owns the ranch."

In a moment they understood what all the commotion was about. Bob and a woman stood in front of what appeared to be an empty stall. But when Doug and Whitney got closer, they could see that a mare lay on her side on the floor.

"And this," Doug said quietly, "is the little lady we came here

143

to see." He turned to Bob. "When did it start?"

Bob glanced at his watch. "We've been here all day. Her sack broke about twenty minutes ago, so it shouldn't be long now."

Whitney knew enough about horses to know they very rarely lie down, usually not even to sleep. The animal in front of her must be sick. And from the serious way the men were talking, it sounded like the horse was on the verge of death.

"What's wrong with her? Is she going to be okay?"

Bob turned to Whitney and smiled. "I'm surprised you don't know, ma'am. You two are kindred spirits, after all."

"What?"

Now the woman turned to her. "Let me apologize for my husband. He forgets to have manners sometimes." She extended her hand. "I'm Bonnie Henderson."

Whitney shook her hand. "Nice to meet you. What's wrong with the horse?"

Bonnie smiled. "Not a thing, dear. She's having a baby."

Whitney looked at the mare and finally took in the whole picture: the shallow breathing, the distended stomach, the huge patch of wet straw beneath the animal. It took Whitney's breath away for a moment. She was actually going to experience the birth of a living creature. But the mother still looked like she was dying.

"Isn't there something we can do to help her?" Whitney asked in concern.

Bonnie shook her head. "Nope. For right now, we just have to stand back and let her do it her way."

Doug patted Whitney's hand in reassurance. "If there are any problems, there's a vet on call. He can jump in at any time. Besides, Bob and Bonnie have been doing this for a long time."

Whitney was glad to know some provisions had been made in case of an emergency. The four of them watched the mare intently, waiting for any sign that the foal was coming.

Finally, Bob elbowed Doug, pointing toward the mare's hindquarters. "Look there. This is it."

Whitney was amazed to see two tiny hooves coming out of the mare, right beneath her tail. They were encased in what looked like a gauzy sack. A few moments later Whitney could make out the foal's tiny muzzle. She was concerned that the foal wouldn't be able to breathe through the sack and was about to say something when it ripped open. As if reading her thoughts, Bonnie put her hand on Whitney's arm and said, "That was supposed to happen. This is a perfectly normal birth. Thank God."

Whitney couldn't utter a word. She just nodded her head. She was too in awe of the miracle unfolding before her. It wasn't long before the newborn foal lay on the straw in front of them. His mother nickered to him, lifted up her head, and began cleaning him off with her huge pink tongue.

And it was done. They all stood back and watched as mother and son acquainted themselves with each other. Eventually, after many failed attempts, the new little foal managed to stand. He teetered on his new matchstick legs, wobbling and weaving, trying desperately to remain standing while his mother continued to lick him dry. The baby rocked to and fro, his head down and his knees locked, determined not to give in to this great force that moved him.

All at once, the humans who had been standing by quietly watching finally jumped into action. They checked the foal and the mother and started to clean out the old straw to replace it with fresh bedding. Whitney was so choked with emotion she didn't know what to do. Eventually she managed to say something.

"Thank you."

Doug turned to her. "What?"

"This was incredible," she said softly. "Thank you for bringing me. For sharing this with me."

"It was the least I could do after all you've shared with me." Her hand rested on the half-top of the stall door. He meant to cover her hand with his for just a moment, as a reassuring gesture. But when he did, she turned her hand over. Their fingers laced together and she squeezed his hand, and they stayed that way for quite a while, watching the new life in front of them trying to figure out this strange new world he'd been born into.

CHAPTER 14

The sound coming from the shower wasn't pretty. In fact, Doug knew his singing was more like a cross between a wail and a yodel. But he couldn't help it. He was happy. Happier than he'd been in a long time, and that made him want to sing. Unfortunately, he couldn't remember all the words to the song.

"I'm on the top of the world—wo, wo, wo—oh yeah, oo, oo—Your love's put me at the top of the world!" He brought his song to a close with a final whoop at the end, then turned his face into the water for one last rinse before turning it off and getting out.

As he stood on the bath mat drying himself with a large fluffy towel, he started to chuckle. "Well, the Bible says to make a joyful noise . . . doesn't say anything about vocal ability."

He opened the bathroom door just a crack to let the steam out. Immediately a host of wonderful smells drifted in from the kitchen. It was Thanksgiving Day, and his mother had been up since dawn cracked, working on a feast. He could make out the spicy cinnamon from the special breakfast rolls she'd made, as well as the aroma of the twenty-five-pound turkey that was already in the oven.

Doug passed his hand across the mirror above the sink, wiping away the condensation and revealing his image. He took a good long look at himself and was pleased with what he saw.

For quite some time, before he'd returned home, Doug had avoided mirrors. He wasn't a vain person, but he was aware of his physical attributes as well as his shortcomings. The problem was, he'd gotten to the point where he didn't even recognize himself when he did see his reflection.

Track life hadn't been easy. He'd set a hard pace, aiming to build up his name and work with better horses at bigger stables. There'd been no time for friends or socializing or keeping in touch with his family. There definitely had been no time for God. Occasionally, one of the jockeys he worked with would pray before a race, but Doug had just chalked that up to superstition. After all, why would God care who won a horse race? It hadn't occurred to him then that the jockey might be praying to survive the race.

The racing game had been exciting and challenging at first. The whole idea of being the best in his field, getting the recognition, standing in the winner's circle, was something that appealed to Doug. He'd made good money too, but that wasn't even the biggest thrill for him. He was looking for validation, for fulfillment. But it always seemed just beyond his reach. It was always one race away.

Then Stan died and Doug had found himself shaken to the core. He hadn't realized until that moment just how much he'd come to rely on Stan, not just in business matters, but as a true and close friend. After the funeral, Doug came back to his hotel room and took a good long look at himself in the mirror. The person looking back was tired, his eyes hard and dull. Where was the satisfaction and fulfillment all his hard work was supposed to have brought him? He must have stood there for twenty minutes, racking his brain, just trying to remember what he used to look like. Who he used to be.

Doug had spent enough time in hotels to be familiar with the amenities, so he knew there'd be a Bible in the bedside table. It had been years since he'd cracked one, but he still remembered some of the old memory verses from Sunday school. He flipped through the thin pages until finally he stumbled onto a verse that read, "What good is it for a man to gain the whole world, yet forfeit his soul?"

It was as though that verse had been written just for him. It finally hit home that the life he was living was empty. Certainly he was becoming well known in his circle and he was making quite a bit of money. But at what price? He'd abandoned his family and his faith. He was empty inside. And that was when he made up his mind to go home.

The Lord had definitely been watching over him that night, because determining to go home was the best decision Doug had ever made. Doug smiled, and his reflection smiled back. Now his eyes were alive, and there was a satisfaction in his expression that had long been missing. It was good to feel like himself again.

Now it was Thanksgiving, and he had so much to be thankful for. Things were going well with his father. Not only had they repaired their relationship, but they were on the brink of starting a successful new business. Doug knew in his heart the joint effort he and his father were putting together would be well received.

And then there was Whitney. As he toweled off and put his clothes on, Doug couldn't stop thinking about her. In all the years they'd known each other, he'd never dreamed that one day she would be the love of his life. But she was.

He was buttoning up his shirt when a twinge of guilt stopped him short. Cliff. He missed his brother like crazy. The only thing that would make this Thanksgiving better was if Cliff was still alive and was with them. But that would mean Doug and Whitney wouldn't be together. Which brought him back to the thought that kept nagging at him. Was it all right to be so happy loving Whitney, when Cliff's death was what had made it possible?

He shook his head and quickly buttoned his shirt the rest of the way. What had happened to Cliff was a tragedy, but there was nothing he could do about it. Surely Cliff wouldn't want Whitney to stop living her life, to stop loving. And if she happened to fall in love with Cliff's brother . . . Doug had heard people say that God works in strange and mysterious ways. This certainly seemed to be an extreme example of that.

"Doug," his mother called from the kitchen. "Get a move on, son. We don't want to be late for church!"

He smiled as a warm wave of nostalgia swept over him. How many times had he heard that growing up? It had been good to be home and staying in his old room, although it had taken a bit of adjusting. And during the start-up phase of the business, it was important for him to be on the premises. Doug knew that his parents liked having him around and would let him stay there as long as he wanted, but he was beginning to get itchy. It was time to start thinking about getting a place of his own. Of course, it was a moot point until after Whitney had the baby. Right now, he needed to be as close to her as possible.

Doug walked into the kitchen. Hank was sitting at his usual spot at the table, reading a livestock magazine and working on his morning cup of coffee, looking like he had all the time in the world. In exact contrast, Myra was a flurry of activity in the kitchen. It was only eight in the morning, yet she'd already made half of Thanksgiving dinner, had the other half waiting in the fridge ready to go, and had a huge breakfast set out at the table. As usual, his mother was amazing. Doug sneaked up behind her and wrapped his arms around her in a bear hug.

"Happy Thanksgiving, Mom."

She turned to him, smiling broadly, and kissed him quickly on the cheek. "And a blessed Thanksgiving to you too." She sniffed a few times, then stood back, putting her hands on her hips, and whistled. "My, my, don't you smell fancy. Trying to impress somebody?"

Doug ran his hand across the back of his neck. He should have known someone would say something. "It's just aftershave, Mom. This is a special day, after all."

She nodded and turned back to the oven. "True," she said while checking on the turkey. "Just don't go around the horses smelling like that. You know how flighty they can be. You might spook them."

"Or make them swoon, one or t'other." Hank Poulten didn't even look up from his reading as he made the offhand comment, but Doug could hear the smile in his father's voice.

Doug was about to answer back that they might want to keep some of the aftershave around for use during breeding season when the bells hanging on the back door jingled. He turned around, expecting to see one of his sisters walk in. What he saw instead did not make him happy.

Whitney stomped her feet on the mat that lay just inside the door, shaking the snow from her feet. Then she sat on the narrow bench, pulled her boots off, and replaced them with a pair of leather loafers she'd carried in a canvas bag.

Myra floated over to her daughter-in-law and kissed her on the cheek. "Hello, hon." She helped Whitney take off her heavy coat and scarf, hanging them on pegs on the wall. It wasn't until Whitney had dispensed with all of her cold weather gear that Doug found his voice.

"Whitney! What do you think you're doing?"

She cocked her head to the side slightly. "What I do every year. I'm coming for Thanksgiving breakfast." She turned away from him and looked at Myra, who had gone back into the kitchen. "Is that okay, Myra?"

"Well, of course it is." The older woman flew out of the kitchen, gave Whitney another quick hug, and moved her over to a seat at the table in one continuous motion. "Douglas, where are your manners?"

Now Hank looked up. "Maybe his brain's being affected by the chemicals in that aftershave."

Whitney sat down next to her father-in-law and leaned in, speaking in a loud stage whisper. "Pretty powerful stuff, huh?"

"You can say that again. Bet we could put it to darn good use during the breeding season."

This was not the way Doug had envisioned the morning. "Okay, I can take a hint. Would you like me to go take another shower?"

"No!" all three shouted in unison.

"You know we were just teasing," Myra called, her head now peering into the refrigerator.

Hank closed his magazine and reached toward the chair on the other side of him. "Set yourself down, son, and have some breakfast." Then he added with a wink, "Your scent will wear off soon enough."

Doug sat across from Whitney. "So," she said, "you never did answer your mother's question."

"I don't even remember what the question was anymore," Doug said in exasperation.

Whitney was only too happy to remind him. "Where did your manners go?"

Doug let out a sigh as he took the plate of sweet rolls his dad handed him. "Look, I didn't mean it the way it came out. It's not that I don't want you here, I just didn't like the way you got here."

Whitney looked confused. "The way I got here? I walked."

"Exactly!" He poked the air with his finger, emphasizing his point. "You shouldn't be doing so much walking in your condition. Especially when the ground is covered with snow and it's freezing outside."

Doug knew the only reason Whitney was staying so calm was

because his parents were in the room. If they'd been alone, she would have blasted him already. "My condition doesn't preclude me from walking. In fact, the doctor says that walking is good for me. As for the weather, it's not that cold outside, and you've kept the path to my house so well cleared that there's hardly any snow on it. Now," she held her hand up, cutting off the remark that Doug was getting ready to make, "it's Thanksgiving, and I'm hungry. So would you please pass the rolls, Dougie?"

The church service was beautiful. As always, Whitney felt complete with Doug standing beside her, holding one side of the hymnal, his enthusiastic voice mingling with hers as they sang. Pastor Rogers's message was particularly poignant. His sermon theme was, " 'In all things give thanks.' " He reminded them that God is the only one who knows the master plan, that even in sorrow, it's important to thank God for the good that he can work from the situation and for the blessings that he's already given.

Whitney didn't look at Doug, but she could feel him next to her. This was one of the blessings that had sprung from tragedy. Her relationship with Doug was completely different from what she'd had with Cliff. It was still difficult for her to reconcile the fact that she could love two men so completely, yet so differently. And it really had nothing to do with them being brothers anymore.

When Whitney and Cliff had married, she knew it would be forever . . . "till death do us part." She had never wanted, needed, or desired anyone else. When he died, she believed that her one true, great love was over. She knew that she would never love again.

But then Doug came home. Slowly, the friendship that had always existed between them turned into another kind of love.

She was older now than when she'd fallen in love with Cliff, so this relationship felt a little more mature, a little more solid. But that fact didn't take anything away from what she and Cliff had shared. At the same time, the love she'd had for Cliff didn't diminish the feelings she had for Doug.

The baby chose that moment to shift positions, reminding her of the most confusing part of this puzzle. How could she be sure what she was feeling for Doug wasn't just some desperate need to be with someone? She was a pregnant widow, her hormones were running amok, and her emotions were more volatile than they'd ever been before. How could she be sure that Shawna hadn't hit the nail on the head? Maybe she was so desperate not to be alone that she had grabbed onto Doug as soon as he'd made himself available.

But then she turned to look at Doug and discovered he was already looking at her. Immediately a smile took over his whole face, from his lips to his eyes. And she knew. She loved this man, and he loved her. It was Thanksgiving Day, and God had given her a great gift to be thankful for. With a contented sigh, Whitney turned her attention back to the pastor's sermon.

"I'm stuffed!"

Whitney settled carefully on her living room sofa. Doug followed her into the house, his arms full of plastic containers.

"Where do you want all this food?"

She motioned toward the kitchen. "Wherever there's room in the fridge. I don't know how I'll eat it all, though. Your mom sent enough to feed an army."

Doug stowed the containers, then came into the front room and sat next to Whitney. "I guess she figures you can use the food since you're eating for two."

"Two what? It's just me and one itty-bitty baby!" She rubbed her stomach lightly and kicked off her flat shoes. "Man, I'm beat."

Doug smiled. "It was a good day, though."

"Oh yeah, a great day. But I'm still beat."

They sat silently for a moment, then both spoke at once.

"Doug . . ."

"Hey, Whit . . ."

Whitney laughed and Doug fiddled with the some imaginary lint on the knee of his pants. "Sorry," he said. "You first."

"Okay. You know, in some ways, obviously, this has been the worst year of my life. But today I focused on all the things that I'm thankful for . . . on all the blessings God's given me." She reached over and took his hand. "And you know, you're right at the top of the list. I'm very thankful that God put you in my life. I want to make sure you know that."

Doug hesitated, as if afraid that any movement he made might make the moment disappear. Then he moved closer and cupped her cheek with his hand. "Ah, Whit," he finally said, "you know how I feel about you."

He leaned in and kissed her. His lips moved softly against hers, and she responded in kind. It was the most tender kiss Whitney had ever experienced, and she gave herself over to the moment, not wanting to think about anything else—until it ended and Doug whispered, almost against her lips, "But we can't do this."

Her eyes flew open and she sat back in shock. "What did you say?"

He gave her a sad smile and shook his head. "I know that's the last thing you expected to hear from me."

"Well, yes, to tell the truth." Whitney felt her cheeks flush red. What a fool she'd just made out of herself. "I just thought . . ." Her words trailed off uncertainly.

Doug squeezed both her hands in his. "Whitney, you thought

right. I love you. God knows I love you more than I ever thought I could love anybody."

She stared at him, perplexed. "I don't understand."

Doug sighed and ran a hand through his hair. "I don't know if I completely understand it, either, but I'll give it a go. This morning I was thinking about how God's worked in my life. I tried my best to run from him, but he was always there, taking care of things whether I knew it or not. And he's still with me. I know God has a plan for you and me, Whitney, and I don't want to mess it up."

Whitney felt her eyes filling, and she was determined not to cry in front of Doug. But a tear escaped and ran down her cheek anyway. He reached up and tenderly brushed it away.

"Darned hormones," she muttered.

A low laugh rumbled in Doug's chest. "That's part of why I want us to wait. Whitney, you've got so much going on right now. You're carrying a little life, and that's a big responsibility. After the baby's born, there will be plenty of time for you and me to pick this up. What do you think?"

She gave him a glimmer of a smile. "You'll wait for me?"

He nodded. "As long as it takes."

She knew he was right, but she still wanted to be close to him. "Would it be okay if you just held me now?"

He opened his arms to her. "Absolutely."

They stayed that way for a while, with her head resting on his chest, and his arms securely around her. Whitney let herself be lulled by the steady, strong beating of Doug's heart. For the first time since he came home, Whitney felt completely at peace. About a month, she thought. In about a month, the baby would be born, and then they could explore this unique new relationship. Until then, she could rest.

CHAPTER 15

"Do you think Sarah would like this?" Whitney made a face as she held up a filmy peasant top with long flowing sleeves. She'd drawn Sarah's name in the annual family Christmas present lottery and had no idea what to get for the young woman.

She looked over at Doug and resisted the temptation to laugh. The poor fellow had agreed to take her Christmas shopping, but had no idea he'd spend most of his time in the women's department of every store in the mall. Now he was staring at nothing in particular, his eyes slightly glazed over.

"Earth to Doug," she intoned while poking him in the arm.

"What?" He instantly turned to her. "What's wrong?"

"Nothing's wrong. I want your opinion." She held up the blouse and wiggled it from side to side.

Now he was clearly uncomfortable. "Well," he started out slowly, "don't you think that top is a little, . . . uh, sheer for you?"

She rolled her eyes. "It's not for me. It's for your sister."

"Oh, well, then, it's definitely too sheer."

Whitney looked at it again, her brows knitting together. "You're supposed to wear a tank top or something under it. I think." She let out an exasperated sigh and hung the blouse back on the rack. "I'm sorry to drag you through this shopping nightmare. I just don't know what to get for Sarah."

"Well why didn't you say so?" He smiled, put his arm around

her shoulders and led her outside. "I know exactly what to get her."

"You do?"

"Sure. A gift certificate."

Twenty minutes later they sat in the food court and Whitney felt extremely satisfied. She had a mall gift certificate in her purse and a plate of lo mein noodles and orange chicken sitting on the table in front of her. Life was good.

A moment later Doug put down his tray and sat across from her. "Whoever came up with the idea of the first food court was a genius," he said as he picked up his sandwich. It was oozing cheese, onions and mushrooms over thin slices of steaming roast beef. "This way you can eat your girlie food, and I can eat something manly."

She laughed as he bit into the sandwich and half of it fell out of the roll and onto his plate. "Since when is Chinese food girly? At least I'm not eating a heart attack on a bun."

He wiggled his eyebrows at her. "But what a way to go!"

They ate for a while before Whitney spoke up. "So, my agent called me again."

"She still wants you to work with that new author?"

Whitney nodded, not taking her eyes off her noodles. "The author and the publisher still think I'm the best choice for the project."

Doug paused to take a drink. "Do you feel any differently about it now?"

"I don't know." Whitney was swirling the lo mein noodles around on her plate with her fork. She hadn't wanted to think too much about the situation, but she knew she wanted Doug's input.

He pushed his tray aside and wiped his hands on a napkin. As she'd expected, Doug gave her his full attention. "I'm assuming you're still hung up on the fact that you've never worked on a book with anybody but Cliff."

"That's the problem right there," she answered, looking up at him. "I know I need to work. . . . I want to work. But I feel disloyal working on a book with somebody else."

"I understand how you feel, but I think you're being too hard on yourself. I mean, you're not cheating on Cliff if you work with another writer."

They were both silent then. The implication of what Doug had said was clear. And you're not cheating on Cliff if you fall in love with me.

"I know you're right," Whitney finally answered. "It's just a weird thing to adjust to. Anyway, I told Gail that I couldn't possibly take on a new project until after the baby's born, so I've got a little time to think it through. Now, let's change the subject. What have you been up to?"

"More of the same. Those horses take up a lot of time." He popped a french fry into his mouth and added casually, "I've also been looking for a new place to live."

This was news to Whitney. "What's wrong with where you live now?"

"Nothing," he said with a shrug, "but it's time to move on. I can't stay with my parents forever, can I?"

"No, I guess not." Whitney knew this shouldn't bother her, but it did. He was a grown man, so of course he'd want a place of his own. On the other hand, it could be a sign that he was getting antsy. If he felt like it was time to move on, he might be getting ready to bolt again.

She looked up as he covered her hand with his. "Whit, are you okay?" He motioned toward her plate with a smile. "You've hardly eaten anything, and I know how much you love that stuff."

"I'm fine," she said with a nod. "My stomach's just a little out of sorts."

His smile vanished. "Out of sorts how?"

She shrugged. "I don't know. I'm not sick to my stomach, I'm just feeling a little . . . crampy, I guess."

"How long have you been feeling crampy?" he asked evenly.

She hesitated before admitting, "Since we got here."

"What?" His response was so loud that several people around them turned to look. "Whitney, we've been here for three hours. And we had to drive over an hour to get here. Don't you remember Janet saying that long car rides during the end of the third trimester can bring on labor? You could be having contractions."

She shook her head and laughed. "Now see, this is why I didn't say anything. I knew you'd jump to conclusions. That thing about the car is just an old wives' tale. Besides, I'm not due for another two weeks. I can't be having contractions."

"Come on." He was on his feet, and before she knew it he'd grabbed her wrist and they were heading for the door.

She looked back at the table. "What about the trays?"

"I think we can be excused from food court etiquette at a moment like this."

"Doug, I really think you're overreacting."

"Whatever you say, Cleopatra. But I'm getting you to a hospital."

"Why did you call me that?"

"Because you're the queen of denial."

She rolled her eyes. "Did you know that you tell really bad jokes when you're nervous?"

He frowned at her. "I'm not nervous. I'm just a lousy joke teller."

Doug stopped short when they reached the door to the parking lot. "You wait here while I get the truck."

Whitney shook her head sharply, frowning at him. This had

gone far enough. "Oh come on, now. I walked in. I can surely walk out."

But Doug wasn't about to give an inch. "I wasn't crazy about you walking in, either. Whitney, be sensible. It's the middle of December. It's freezing outside and there's ice on the ground. The last thing we need is for you to slip and fall." He wasn't making much headway until he added, "At least think of the baby."

Darn him, she thought. He knows my Achilles' heel. "Oh, all right," she gave in. "I'll wait here."

He smiled. "Great. You just sit tight, and I'll be right back."

At that point, they both looked around and realized that, thanks to the Christmas rush, there wasn't a seat to be had. Anticipating Doug's next move, Whitney put her hand on his arm and said softly, "It's okay. I can stand."

But he quickly moved to the bench nearest the door, which was full of teenagers. "Excuse me," he boomed loudly enough to be heard over their laughter.

They all turned to look at him. One boy, whose buzz-cut hair was dyed green and red, was obviously the alpha-teen. "Hey, man," he spoke slowly, "we're not bothering anybody."

"No, you're not. In fact, I was hoping you could help me." He reached back for Whitney's arm and pulled her forward. "Would you please let my friend sit down?"

None of them said a word. They just looked at Whitney as if she was the first pregnant woman in the history of mall shopping. Doug went on. "She's having a baby." Still no response. "She's having the baby right now!"

That got a reaction out of them. The air was suddenly filled with "Dude" and "No way!" and every one of them jumped off the bench as if she might explode right in front of them.

Whitney would have been thrilled if the mall floor had opened and swallowed her up right then. But instead she apologized.

"I'm sorry. My friend's really overreacting. I'm not—" She broke off in midsentence as another cramp hit her. This one was worse than the others. In fact, it rather took her breath away. "Oh, wow, maybe I should sit down."

Before she knew it, she was being led to the bench, Doug on one side, and a girl with a pierced nose on the other. "Thanks," she whispered.

The boy with the red and green hair spoke up. "Dude, you get your car. We'll watch out for your lady."

"Are you going to be okay till I get back?" Doug asked Whitney.

"Sure," she answered. "Just go."

Doug nodded and ran for the door. Another boy dressed all in black, except for a floppy felt elf hat, followed him. "I'll be the lookout," he called back. "I'll let you know when he brings the ride around."

Whitney looked at the motley bunch she'd been left with. Now that she thought the baby really might be coming, she was glad there were people with her. Even if they were the most interesting people she'd ever met.

Nobody said anything at first. Finally Whitney decided it would be good to break the ice. "My name's Whitney."

"I'm Ron," the boy with the buzz cut answered.

"Zoë," said the girl with the nose ring.

"Jake." This voice was behind her, so Whitney wasn't sure what he looked like.

Ron perched himself on the arm of the bench and faced her. "The guy that ran off with your husband is Otis."

Whitney felt her face flush. She hated having to explain her situation. "He's not my husband."

Ron held up his hand. "Dude, it's cool. Whatever works for you."

She knew this group of kids wouldn't sit in judgment, but

she also didn't want to give them the wrong impression. "My husband's dead. Doug, the man I'm with today, is a very good friend. He's helped me a lot."

For some reason, her admission touched the kids more than she would have expected. Jake came around the bench and sat on the floor in front of her. Zoë sat down next to her and put her hand on her shoulder. "Man, that's so harsh. How did he die?"

Whitney was surprised that a stranger would ask such a personal question, but she answered anyway. "He was in a plane crash."

Zoë nodded. "My dad died in a logging accident."

Ron looked across the mall as he said, "Cancer took my mom out."

Jake was sitting cross-legged with his head hanging down, so she barely heard him murmur, "My sister OD'd."

Whitney could hardly believe the pain that surrounded her. "You've all lost somebody?"

Ron nodded. "That's how we met. We're all part of a grief group at the youth center in town."

"We're kinda having a hard time with the holiday," Zoë said. "So our counselor suggested we do something to 'embrace' it." She crooked her fingers in the air when she said the word "embrace."

Jake looked up. "Best thing we could come up with was to dress funny and watch people go present-crazy at the mall."

Now Whitney understood Ron's multicolored hair and Otis's elf hat. She also noticed that Zoë wore large dangly earrings made out of tinsel, and Jake had a big Santa face tattooed on his arm. She hoped that one would wash off.

Whitney smiled at them. "You all look very festive. Is it working? Do you feel any better?"

Ron shrugged. "We always feel better when we're together,

you know? We can hang out and laugh and have a great time. But when we're done . . ."

"It's going home that's the hard part," Zoë finished. "Then you can't ignore it anymore. It's right in your face, and there's nothing to do but think about it."

"But not everybody's easy to be around, either," said Jake.

Whitney nodded. "I know what you mean. Right after Cliff died, I used to dread being around our friends. They always wanted to know how I was doing, and then things would get awkward. They meant well, but they just didn't know what to say. So I tried to keep to myself and stay at home, but then I'd just think about Cliff all the time and go crazy missing him."

"And why do people always bring food?" Zoë threw her hands in the air. She was obviously quite passionate about the subject. "Is there some kind of magic in a casserole? And Jell-O salad. What's the deal with that? Why do people think you'll eat food after somebody dies that you wouldn't think of touching on a good day?"

"Grief sucks," Ron said flatly.

Whitney couldn't agree more. She was sorry these three had to find that out so young. "Yeah, but it's a good thing you've got each other. What got me through it was my family and my faith in God."

Next to her, Zoë snorted. "God? Your husband's dead. How can you still believe in God? I mean, if there is a God, he's pretty mean letting so much bad stuff happen in the world."

Oh boy, Whitney thought, here's the thing we all struggle with. "You know, Zoë, I thought that way too, right after Cliff died. But it was just because I was so hurt. Then I realized that bad things happen in this world because God lets people make choices. He's not some puppet master sitting upstairs pulling strings. So sometimes things go wrong. But he also blesses us. For example, God knew I was going to need friends around me today, so he gave me four new ones."

That got a shy smile out of the girl. "Yeah, maybe."

Another contraction hit Whitney. She wanted to double over, but she remembered the breathing exercises she'd learned. So instead she started panting in short, shallow breaths.

Jake sat up on his knees, concern all over his face. "Lady, are you okay?"

She nodded and got out the word "contraction" in between pants. When it was over, she realized they'd all been panting with her and that Ron and Zoë had each taken one of her hands. "Thanks, guys. That was the worst yet."

A shadow fell over them, like something out of a western. I must really be getting loopy, Whitney thought. But when she looked up, there was a security guard, hands on his hips, looking very stern.

"Ma'am, are these kids bothering you?"

The young people around her stiffened and Whitney could practically see them putting their walls back up. Her first instinct was to be indignant. How dare he assume the teens were troublemakers just because of the way they dressed? But then she realized that he was just doing his job. After all, if she hadn't spent some time with them, she might have thought the same thing.

She shook her head and smiled. "No. I'm just hanging out with my friends."

An expression of surprise passed quickly over his face, then he nodded. "Sorry to take your time, then. You all have a happy holiday."

As he walked off, the kids seemed to relax. "Does that happen often?" Whitney asked.

"You mean people judging us because of the way we look?" Zoë shrugged. "Often enough. But if that's the way they think, who needs them?"

"Here's something to think about," Whitney said. "There are all kinds of ways to shut ourselves off from people. For me, it was my work. Whenever someone would try to get me out, I'd say I was too busy, that I had too much work to do. Maybe you guys dress the way you do to keep people away."

Jake seemed to bristle at this. "Or maybe we just like the way we look," he challenged.

Whitney didn't let it faze her. "If that's the case, then fine. All I'm saying is, you seem like really great kids, and I'm glad I got to spend some time with you. I'd hate for other people not to know how great you are just because they couldn't get past the packaging."

As if on cue, the mall doors flew open dramatically and Otis ran in, out of breath and covered with a dusting of snow.

He slid to a stop in front of their bench. "He's right outside in the truck. We'll help you get there."

Ron helped Whitney get to her feet, and the four of them surrounded her as they walked carefully to the door. Otis, in his eagerness to be of assistance, kept shouting, "Make way! Lady with a baby!"

The wind outside was biting, and snow flurries swirled in the air. The harsh winter the old-timers had been predicting had arrived at last. Jake opened the passenger-side door for her. Doug was waiting inside the warm cab, and she wanted nothing more than to get in beside him, but there was one more thing she needed to do first.

"Zoë," she said turning to the girl, "do you know what your name means?"

Zoë shook her head.

"It means 'love.' I just want you to know that you're loved. All of you. Thank you so much for helping me today." She hugged them all, first Zoë, who hugged her back tightly, then each of the boys, who were a little stiff, as if unsure what to do.

When she got to Ron, he kissed her hand and made a little bow.

"Your chariot awaits, m'lady." With a flourish he helped her into the truck.

"Thanks for everything," Doug called out to them. "You guys were great."

Then Jake spoke up. "Where are you going?"

"Holy Angels Hospital," Whitney answered. Another contraction started and she gripped her stomach. "We'd better be getting there fast," she said, turning to Doug.

He made sure her seat belt was buckled and then drove off. Whitney looked up, and in the rearview mirror she could see her four guardian teen angels jumping up and down and waving like crazy.

CHAPTER 16

Kathleen Noel Poulten was born at 12:05 a.m. just two weeks before Christmas. As Whitney looked down at the sleeping baby, she was once again overcome with awe. This little person had lived within her for nine months, and now her daughter was sleeping peacefully in her arms. How different this moment was from the hours preceding the little girl's birth.

Doug had delivered her to the hospital as fast as he could, considering the weather conditions. Still, by the time he pulled up to the curb by the hospital's emergency entrance, the contractions were coming hard and fast. Almost as soon as she came through the door, a young orderly had her settled on a gurney. She'd had only a second to squeeze Doug's hand before they wheeled her off to the labor room. The last she'd seen of Doug, he'd been approached by a clipboard-wielding nurse who was saying something about admission forms.

Whitney thought about how God had watched over her the whole time. Just the fact that she and Doug had been at the mall was a miracle. Her home was well over an hour away from the hospital on a good day, and the bad weather would have made the roads treacherous. But it had taken them only twenty minutes over plowed roads to get to the hospital from the mall. If she'd been at home, there was a good chance they wouldn't have made it in time.

Of course, Katie had waited until after midnight to make her appearance. It was rather symbolic, Whitney thought. This was a new day, and the beginning of a whole new chapter of her life.

Whitney heard a light tapping on the door and then it opened slowly. Doug's grinning face appeared.

"Can I come in?" he asked quietly.

"Of course you can." Whitney smiled and motioned to him with her free hand. "I was wondering where you were."

Doug walked over and sat on the edge of the bed so he could face her and the baby. "You won the bet," he said.

"What bet?"

"Whether it was a boy or a girl. You won fair and square." With that he reached into his jacket and pulled out a king-size chocolate bar.

Whitney laughed. "I don't remember there being an official bet, but you know I won't turn that away."

They sat smiling at each other for a while until Doug looked back down at Katie. "Wow." His hushed tone was almost reverent. "I still can't get over how tiny she is."

"Don't let her size fool you," Whitney answered with a grin. "She's got a powerful set of lungs. When she's hungry, the entire state of Montana will know about it. But how about you? Did you get any sleep at all last night?"

"Oh yeah," he said easily. "You'd be surprised how comfortable the waiting room couches are."

"I'm sure." She covered his hand with hers. "Thank you so much for staying with me . . . with us. It meant a lot knowing you were out there."

He raised her hand to his lips and gave it a gentle kiss. "You know I wouldn't have been anywhere else."

Whitney felt her face flush. Her whole body tingled just from his one innocent gesture. Why did she always feel guilty every time Doug expressed his feelings to her? Gently she pulled her hand back under the pretense of shifting Katie to her other arm. "What about your parents?" she asked, searching for a way to change the subject. "Have you told them the good news?"

"I called after I'd finished filling out your paperwork. They wanted to know as soon as the baby was born, so I called them right after midnight too." He glanced at his watch. "I'm surprised they're not here by now."

"They're coming?" Whitney asked in alarm. "Now?"

Doug chuckled. "Them and every other Poulten in driving distance. Is that a problem?"

"Oh, no," Whitney said sarcastically. "I've always wanted them to see me sleep deprived, with scraggly hair and no makeup. I don't even have a toothbrush!"

"Calm down." Doug spoke in a soothing tone as he patted her arm. "There's a gift shop downstairs. I'm sure they sell toothbrushes. You can't be the first patient to end up at the hospital without an overnight bag. I'll go down and get you a few things."

Whitney relaxed. "Would you? Thank you so much." She counted off the items she'd need on her fingers. "I'd like a toothbrush, toothpaste, and a hairbrush."

Doug stood up and gave her a mock salute. "Your wish is my command."

"Oh, and some lip balm."

"Got it."

"And some ponytail holders if they have them. My hair is bugging me."

"I'd better write this down."

Doug fished a notepad and pen out of his jacket. A few minutes and several additions to the list later, he left Whitney's room in search of toiletries.

Whitney watched as the door swung shut behind him. She looked down at Katie who was still, miraculously, asleep in her arms. "Your Uncle Doug is the best."

Uncle Doug. It just didn't feel right when she said it.

Although it was true, he was Katie's uncle. But Whitney wanted him to have a much greater part in Katie's life. In both their lives.

"But why can't I get past the guilt?" she asked herself.

Again, there was a knock on the door, but this time it was loud and repetitive. Doug couldn't be done shopping already. Maybe he'd forgotten something.

"Come in," she called.

To her amazement, the room was quickly filled with four noisy, excited teenage bodies. Her guardian teen angels.

Zoë ran right up to her, but as soon as she saw Katie she whirled around on the others and shushed them loudly. "Shhh! The baby's trying to sleep!"

Whitney couldn't help but smile. If that didn't wake Katie up, nothing would.

"I hope you don't mind us being here," Zoë continued. "We just had to find out how everything went."

Whitney had a feeling that Zoë probably coerced the rest of the group into joining her, but it meant something that they'd given in and come. "Of course I don't mind. I'm glad you came. Pull up a chair or part of the bed."

Zoë perched in the same place Doug had sat earlier. Ron lounged in the chair beside the bed, while Jake and Otis chose to stand. Whitney looked them over and noticed they'd gotten rid of most of their Christmas accessories. Zoë had replaced her tinsel earrings with big silver hoops, Otis was wearing a normal blue and yellow ski cap, and, thankfully, Jake's tattoo had been temporary; there wasn't a trace of it left. Ron, on the other hand, seemed to like his hair the way it was because it was still bright green and red.

"I see you got rid of your Christmas trappings," she said. "Are you giving up on experiencing holiday cheer?"

"Just the opposite," Ron said.

Whitney raised a questioning eyebrow, and Zoë continued. "We felt so good yesterday helping you out, it made us realize that we may have been doing this grieving thing all wrong. Maybe we've been too into ourselves to let go of the pain."

Otis nodded. "It's kind of hard to stop hurting when all you do is think about it all the time."

"So you're going to look outside of yourself," Whitney answered. "That's great. Have you decided how you're going to do it?"

"We're going to try to do things for other people and with other people." Zoë was so excited she was almost bouncing up and down on the bed. "Like last night, instead of shutting myself in my room, I spent time with my Mom. I've been so wrapped up in how bad I felt that I never thought about how much she was hurting too. We had a good talk."

"The youth center hosts a holiday dinner for the needy every Christmas," Ron said. "Otis and I are going to work it this year."

"That's great," Whitney said enthusiastically. "How about you, Jake?"

The entire time, Jake had been standing silently with his hands stuffed in the pockets of his jeans and his head hung low. Now he just shrugged and answered, "I haven't decided yet."

Whitney's heart broke for him. She remembered that his sister had died of an overdose. To Jake, it probably felt like she had chosen to leave him. For the others, accidents or disease were at fault. Of the four of them, Jake would have the hardest time dealing with his loss and moving on. But with God's grace and the support of his family and friends, she knew he could do it.

"That's okay," Whitney said. "You don't have to come up with all the answers in one day. It sounds like you're all on the right track though."

There was an awkward moment when none of them knew what to say. Luckily Zoë never stayed quiet for very long. "Your baby's so pretty. What's her name?"

"Kathleen Noel. 'Kathleen' means 'dear to my heart' and I guess I don't have to explain 'Noel.' "

Jake surprised them all by saying, "It's too bad her father can't see her."

Whitney felt heat building up behind her eyes, but she blinked several times, determined not to cry in front of them. "You know, Jake, I think he can. Cliff was a believer, so I know he's in heaven. I'll bet you anything he's looking down right now, smiling at her."

"Do they ever stop looking down?" Otis asked. "Do you think they ever go on with their eternal lives so we can go on with ours?"

The seriousness of his question took her aback. It was something she hadn't really thought much about before. "Yes," she answered carefully. "I think they do. I think God lets us feel the presence of our loved ones as long as we need it. And when we're ready to move on, God helps us with that."

"Like your boyfriend," Ron added. "It was pretty cool of God to put him in your life when you needed him."

This time she didn't correct Ron. Maybe she wouldn't have called Doug her boyfriend, but the meaning was the same. Doug was very special to her. And it was pretty cool of God to bring them together.

The movement in her arms diverted her attention. Katie was waking up. Whitney had only been with her daughter for a few hours, but it was long enough for her to know what was coming.

"I hate to kick you guys out," she said, "but Katie's going to need to eat soon."

They looked at her blankly. Whitney smiled to herself. Obvi-

173

ously she was going to have to spell it out for them. "I'm breast-feeding."

She'd never seen four people leave a room so fast. Zoë sprang from the bed and kissed her on the cheek. Ron gave her shoulder a quick squeeze. Otis and Jake just waved from where they stood, and then they were all gone. Just in the nick of time too, because Katie was starting to cry.

"Hold on, now," Whitney said softly. "Let's both get comfy and then you can eat."

It took Whitney a moment to get the pillow situated behind her and adjust her gown, but finally Katie got her breakfast. Whitney looked down at the nursing infant. She had never felt so satisfied in her entire life. Everything was perfect . . . almost.

She thought about the teenagers and what they'd discussed. Without even knowing it, they had nailed her problem. It seemed God had put them into her life for more than one reason.

It had been eight months since Cliff died, and all that time she'd convinced herself that she was doing okay, that she was moving on. But she hadn't really finished grieving. She'd never really and truly let Cliff go.

Now she knew that moving on with her life didn't mean that she loved Cliff any less. No matter what happened in her future, the fact would remain that she and Cliff had shared a deep love. The proof of that was in her arms. But she didn't have to be tied to a memory. Especially not when she was loved by someone who was flesh and blood.

"Oh God," she prayed out loud, "Now I see it. Thank you for giving me all those wonderful years with Cliff. Thank you for the love we shared and for our beautiful child. But I'm ready to move on now. You've given me a second chance to feel love and be loved. I want to embrace that. I don't want to run anymore."

She looked down at Katie. The baby had finished nursing,

and was now happily gurgling in Whitney's arms. "Hello, precious," she said to her daughter. "You didn't get to know your father, but he was a wonderful man. I promise to do everything I can to help you get to know who he was. I'm always going to love your father and he'll always have a place in my heart."

For the first time since Cliff's accident, Whitney broke down and sobbed. She'd had to be strong for so long. At first, she was strong for Cliff's parents. Then when she found out she was pregnant, she'd been strong for the baby. She'd had her moments of sniffling and a tear or two, but now she allowed herself really to cry. And when she finished, it felt as though all the pain and hurt was washed out of her soul.

There was another light tapping on the door and then a nurse entered, rolling in what looked like a clear plastic bassinet. Whitney quickly wiped her eyes with the back of one hand, but her tears didn't worry the nurse. She apparently saw a lot of them.

"How are you two girls doing?" she asked pleasantly.

"Wonderful," Whitney said. "Katie just finished breakfast."

The nurse looked down at her watch. "More like brunch, I'd say. What about you, Mommy? I'll bet you're ready for a little break."

Whitney shook her head. "Oh, no, I'm fine, really."

The nurse nodded and smiled. "That may be, but you won't be any good to that little girl of yours if you don't take care of yourself. Right now you need some rest. My advice is to take advantage of the time you're in the hospital and sleep as much as you can. The good Lord knows you won't get much sleep once you go home!"

"I guess you're right." Reluctantly, Whitney let the nurse take Katie from her arms. She watched the woman gently lay the baby in the bassinet and then check her blanket. Whitney knew her child was in good hands.

The nurse turned back to her. "Don't worry about a thing. Just get a couple hours of rest. When you wake up, you can buzz me and I'll bring her back when you're ready."

Whitney nodded and watched as the nurse wheeled her daughter out of the room. The door shut behind them with a soft swoosh, and the room suddenly felt very empty and quiet. Whitney switched on the TV, just to have some sound in the room, but she quickly turned it back off. She was in no mood to listen to mindless talk-show banter or empty infomercial promises. There were more important things on her mind.

She wished Doug were back. Everything was so clear to her now. All that was left was to tell Doug. More than anything, Whitney wanted to talk to him and tell him how she felt. She was finally ready to start their life together.

Chapter 17

"Hold the elevator!"

Doug ran down the hospital corridor and called out just as the doors were beginning to close. If he tried to push the call button, he would drop all the stuff he was carrying, so he was relieved when the doors slid back open.

"Thanks," Doug said, stepping inside.

"No problem," answered the man in the elevator. "Fourth floor?"

"Yes," Doug answered in surprise. "How'd you know?"

The man pointed at the enormous teddy bear under Doug's left arm. "Fourth floor is maternity. I'm headed there too. This your first?"

Doug's heart swelled with emotion. Was this his first baby? "Yes, it is."

The man nodded sagely. "See, I could tell. When we had our first, I was just like you. Every time we had another one, I got the baby a smaller animal." He held up his empty hands. "This time, no animal. We've got so many at home, the kids just pass them around."

The elevator stopped to let more passengers on, so Doug and his companion moved over to make room.

"How many children do you have?" Doug asked.

"Five," the man said, his tone resigned. "We had three, which I thought was a great number. But Marge—she's my wife—she wanted one more. Just one more, she said. Wouldn't you know it, this time we had twins."

Doug chuckled and the man next to him managed a grin, but he still looked dog tired.

"That's a lot of kids," Doug said.

The man nodded. "Yep. I wouldn't trade one of them. But sometimes I do wish they could already drive themselves around."

The elevator stopped at the fourth floor and they got out. "Good luck to you," Doug said.

"You too. And enjoy the new baby. There's nothing like your first one."

Doug walked toward Whitney's room, his mind whirling. He'd been so concerned about Whitney that he'd never stopped to think of how this baby affected him. He loved Whitney with all his heart and planned to marry her as soon as she'd have him. So Katie was going to be his child. His first child had just been born. The revelation hit him in the pit of his stomach, but it wasn't a bad feeling. A huge grin spread over his face and he started to walk faster. He had to get to Whitney's room. He'd told her that he would be patient and wait until after the baby was born. Well, Katie was here now, so there was no reason why he and Whitney had to wait any longer. Now they could finally be together.

He rounded a corner and almost ran into a group of kids also walking at top speed. It took him a moment before he recognized them.

"Hey," he said. "It's you guys!"

Apparently they didn't recognize him, either, because they all took up a defensive stance. Arms crossed, weight shifted to one hip, sullen expressions. . . . They had it down pat.

"Yeah," Ron said with heavy attitude. "It's us. Who are you?"

Doug shifted the teddy bear in his arms so they could get a better look at him. "Doug. From last night at the mall."

The change that came over all of them was immediate. They were suddenly more open, and two of them even smiled. "Oh yeah," Zoë answered. "You're Whitney's boyfriend."

Doug smiled and nodded. "You could say that." But hopefully, he thought, I'll be her fiancé in a few minutes.

Ron spoke up. "We just left her room. Dude, be careful. She was just getting ready to feed the baby."

He spoke as if it was a government secret. Then Zoë whispered, "You know, breast-feeding." They all nodded gravely.

Doug refrained from laughing. After all the help they'd given, he definitely didn't want to embarrass these kids. "Thanks for the warning. I'll be very careful."

They exchanged good-byes, and then Doug was once more on his way to Whitney's room.

When he got there, the door was cracked open. He didn't want to burst in on her, especially if she was still feeding Katie, so he shifted the packages again, trying to free a hand to knock on the door. Then he heard her voice, and it stopped him cold.

"You didn't get to know your father, but he was a wonderful man. I promise to do everything I can to help you get to know who he was. I'm always going to love your father and he'll always have a place in my heart."

And then she began to cry. Not just a little, but big heart-wrenching sobs that came from the depths of her soul. All the joy Doug had felt just a moment before vanished. He backed away from the door slowly, quietly, and went to the waiting area around the corner.

Doug dropped heavily onto the couch and let the packages fall from his hands. She didn't love him. Had she known all this time that they would never be together? Had she told him to wait just so she wouldn't be alone during her pregnancy?

Doug shook his head sharply. No, Whitney wouldn't do something like that. She'd always been honest with him. She'd told him that her feelings were mixed up, and she needed to wait until after the baby was born to make a rational decision about their future. Doug saw now that she had been right.

How could he have been so stupid? Of course she loved Cliff. Cliff was everything he could never be. Cliff had been solid. He hadn't run off to find fame and fortune on a racetrack. Cliff hadn't abandoned his faith and his family. Doug knew he was a different man today than when he'd left home, but even so, how could he ever hope to compare to Cliff?

He looked up to see a nurse wheeling a baby past him and back to the nursery. He didn't even have to see her close up to know it was Katie. His heart ached. He longed to stop the nurse, to ask to hold the baby, but he couldn't. He had no right.

Wasn't this the supreme irony? He'd finally gotten his life together. He'd stopped running, wanted to set down roots and have a family of his own. But the woman he loved would rather stay tied to a ghost than give him a chance. He supposed it was no more than he deserved.

From far down the hall, Doug could hear a group of people talking animatedly. From the sounds of their voices he knew it was the rest of his family coming to visit Whitney. He stood up and composed himself. There was no way he could let them see that anything was bothering him.

His mother was the first to reach him. "Isn't it exciting!" she said, enfolding him in a bear hug. "Whitney's a mommy! How is she?"

Doug hugged her back. "She's great, Mom. But the nurse just took the baby to the nursery, so I think she's trying to get some rest."

"Oh dear," Myra said. "We don't want to disturb her."

"Why don't we go to the nursery and look at the baby?" Hank suggested.

"Then can we go to the cafeteria?" Jeannie pleaded. "I'm starving."

Sarah perked up at the mention of it. "Ooh, that's a good idea."

Doug nodded. "I think so too. By the time you're done, Whitney should be ready to see you."

"I suppose you're right," Myra said. "But why you would want to eat in a hospital cafeteria is beyond me. They're not known for their food, you know."

Hank winked at his wife. "But they are known for young doctors."

Sarah rolled her eyes and Jeannie blushed, but neither of them contradicted their father.

Doug held up his hand before they could go anywhere. "Wait one second. Can you take these for me?" He picked up the bags, handing them to his dad, and gave the bear to Sarah. "Give these to Whitney when you see her, okay?"

Myra looked perplexed. "Why don't you give them to her yourself? You're coming with us, aren't you?"

"No, Mom. I've got some things I need to take care of." They were all looking at him expectantly, waiting for him to give them an explanation that made sense. But he didn't have one. And he didn't want to answer any more questions. With a wave to his family, Doug turned back down the hall and walked toward the elevators, not entirely sure what he was going to do next.

"Knock, knock."

Whitney was just starting to wake up when she heard the voice at her door. The soft, gentle sing-song could only be Myra Poulten. Great, Whitney thought. The family's all here and I don't have a toothbrush yet.

"Come in," she called.

For the second time that day, her room was filled with people, but this time, they wasted no time in gathering around her. Jeannie and Sarah sat on either side of her bed, while Myra leaned over to kiss her cheek. Hank gave her foot a gentle squeeze through the covers, then sat down in the chair next to the bed. The only one missing was Doug.

"We just came from the nursery," Myra said. "Our granddaughter is gorgeous."

Whitney smiled. "She is, isn't she? It's still all sinking in that I have a daughter."

"Wait till she cries at two in the morning," Sarah said wryly. "Then it'll sink in."

From the other side of the bed, Jeannie gave her sister a shove. "Real encouraging," she said.

"What?" Sarah asked, offended. "It's not like Whitney doesn't think the baby will cry." She turned to Whitney. "Right?"

Whitney nodded with a grin. "Oh yeah, she cries all right. It's a good thing for me I work at home. Hopefully we can both get on the same semisleep schedule."

The entire time they'd been in her room, Sarah had been holding a huge stuffed bear, but nobody said anything about it. Finally, Whitney's curiosity got the best of her. "That wouldn't happen to be for Katie, would it?" she asked Sarah, pointing to the bear.

"Oh, yeah." Sarah thrust the animal out to Whitney.

It was the softest thing Whitney had ever held. "Thanks. I'm sure Katie will adore it."

"It's not from me, though," Sarah hurried to add. "It's from Doug."

"Really?" Whitney found it odd that Doug would get a present for the baby and not bring it in himself.

Hank got up from the chair, holding up two large plastic shopping bags. "He asked us to give you these things too."

She hadn't even noticed that Hank had brought the bags in with him. From the writing on them, Whitney knew they were from the hospital gift shop. They must be the things Doug said he'd get for her. Now she was really confused. "Where is Doug?"

Myra hesitated, then answered, "I'm not really sure, dear. He said he had something to take care of."

"Maybe he's planning a surprise for you," Jeannie suggested hopefully.

Whitney smiled weakly. "Maybe." But she didn't believe it. Something was wrong. Doug had been at the hospital with her from the moment they arrived last night. There was no way he would leave without saying good-bye, even if he was planning something.

"Don't worry yourself, sugar," Hank said. "I'm sure he'll be back soon."

"Oh, I'm not worried." Whitney forced herself to sound bright and cheerful. "I guess I'm still just dog tired."

"Of course you are," Myra answered. "It'd be a miracle if you weren't. We'll all clear out of here so you can get some sleep. And don't worry about a thing. We'll get your place all ready for when you and the baby come home."

"Thanks, Mom," Whitney gave the woman a kiss on the cheek. Then the rest of the family took turns kissing her good-bye.

When they were gone, Whitney looked through the bags. Not only had Doug gotten her the things she'd asked for, but he'd added quite a few things to the list. There were honey-roasted cashews, three different flavors of lip balm, mints, a book of crossword puzzles, a package of mechanical pencils, a novel by one of her favorite authors, and several magazines. Doug had gone to a lot of trouble picking all these things out for her. Not to mention the enormous bear that now took up half of her bed. Why on earth wouldn't he take the time to give them to her?

Calm down, Whitney told herself. Just because he doesn't spend every minute with you doesn't mean there's something wrong. He probably wanted to go home and change his clothes so he'd be fresh.

That must be it. She'd taken a fairly long nap, so he probably thought it was a good time to go change. Rather than dwell on what might be going on, she decided to make herself presentable so that when he did come back, she wouldn't look as weary as she felt. But first she wanted to check on Katie.

It didn't take long after she pressed the call button for a nurse to enter her room. It was the same nurse who had taken Katie earlier.

"I was wondering if you could bring Katie back in," Whitney asked.

The nurse smiled. "When I saw your call light, I figured that's what you wanted, so I swung by the nursery first. Your baby's sleeping right now. Why don't we let her finish her nap, and I'll bring her in as soon as she wakes up. Okay?"

Whitney nodded. "That's fine. And it'll give me a chance to freshen up. I feel pretty grungy."

The nurse laughed. "I'm sure you do. Listen, there's a shower in your bathroom. If you're very careful, you can wash up too. And there are fresh gowns on the shelf next to the towels. They're not pretty, but they're clean."

"Thanks," Whitney answered.

After the nurse left, Whitney gingerly got out of bed and shuffled to the bathroom. Her legs were still a little unsteady, but she could manage it. When she got into the small bathroom, she sat down on the closed toilet seat lid and looked at the miniscule shower. The nurse had told her to be careful. That's the same thing Doug had said the first day he was back. How far they'd come in a few short months.

Twenty minutes later, she was back in the hospital bed wearing a fresh blue gown, her hair hanging clean and wet across her shoulders. Ten minutes after that, the nurse brought Katie to see her. She held Katie for a long time, talking to her and singing. Then she laid Katie in the bassinet the nurse had left beside her bed. She did some crossword puzzles, ate some nuts, flipped halfheartedly through the magazines. At seven p.m. her dinner arrived. At eight p.m. the nurse came to take Katie back to the nursery for the night. As she sat alone in the quiet of her room, Whitney realized with sickening certainty that Doug was not coming back. Definitely not that night, and maybe not ever.

CHAPTER 18

Three weeks later, Whitney sat curled up on her couch with a manuscript propped on her knees. No matter how hard she tried, though, she couldn't read past the first page. Her mind kept going over how much everything had changed since Katie was born.

Her last hope of seeing Doug at the hospital was the day she was released. But he wasn't the one who came to pick her up. Instead, Hank, Jeannie, and Sarah had arrived to help her get her things together and take her home. When they got back to her house, Myra was waiting inside.

"I hope you don't mind me not coming to the hospital, dear," she said, "but I wanted to finish getting everything ready here."

Myra had done a fantastic job. The bassinet was set up in the bedroom and there was a large supply of diapers, baby wipes, and other necessities by the changing table. She'd even stocked Whitney's fridge with home cooked meals.

"All you have to do is pop them in the microwave," she'd said with a smile. "I didn't figure you'd feel like cooking anytime soon."

As much as Whitney appreciated everything they'd done, she couldn't help but be disappointed. She'd imagined the day so differently. She had looked forward to coming home from the hospital with Doug and Katie, all three of them walking through the door together to start the next part of their lives. It wasn't at all the way she'd hoped it would be.

But she didn't have time to dwell on it. Over the next few days, Whitney started to figure out her daughter. Katie definitely had different cries for "I'm hungry" and "I need to be changed." Sleep was another matter. At night, Katie never slept for more than two hours before she woke up wanting to eat. Whitney quickly learned that if she wanted to get any sleep at all, she had to nap with her daughter.

Before she knew it, Christmas had arrived. She prepared for their visit to the Poulten house with a mixture of excitement and trepidation. It would be the first time in two weeks that she'd see Doug. Hopefully, she'd get a chance to talk to him and figure out what was going on.

But when she and Katie arrived, they were greeted by every member of the family except one.

"Where's Doug?" she asked as casually as she could.

Myra was visibly disappointed as she answered. "He's not going to be here. Can you believe it? His first Christmas back home, and he's going to miss it."

"He went to Kalispell to check out some stock," Hank added. "The weather got so bad, he didn't want to take a chance driving the roads. Now, let me hold that precious granddaughter of mine."

The subject quickly changed to Katie. They talked about how much she'd grown and how pretty she was. Whitney told them anecdotes about waking up in the middle of the night and being so sleepy that one day she grabbed hand soap instead of shampoo in the shower. But during it all, Whitney's happiness was tempered by the fact that Doug had chosen to miss Christmas with his family rather than see her.

But Whitney knew from experience that it didn't do any good to sit around wishing for things. It was time she got on with her life, and part of that meant supporting herself and her daughter. The day after Christmas, Whitney had called her agent and told her she was interested in working with the author she had suggested. Gail was thrilled and had promised to send Whitney the manuscript via overnight mail.

So now Whitney sat, reading page one for the umpteenth time. It wasn't the writer's fault. Whitney knew that under normal circumstances she would have enjoyed what she was reading. But she just couldn't focus.

Doug had decided he didn't want to be a part of her life. That was a fact and she knew she'd have to resign herself to it. Whitney just wished she knew why. He'd been so determined that they belonged together, so sincere in expressing his love for her. Why would his feelings suddenly change? Maybe Shawna had been right all along. Maybe Doug had mistaken a sense of duty for love, and after Katie was born, he realized that he'd made a mistake.

The clock on the mantle chimed the hour, pulling Whitney from her reverie. Ron and the rest of her teenage friends had invited her to a pre-New Year's celebration at the Youth Center. Since their meeting at the mall, they had adopted her as part of their circle, and Whitney was happy to be included. It would do her good to get out and be around people instead of moping. If she was going to get there on time, she had to start getting herself and Katie ready.

She looked into the bassinet beside her. Katie was gurgling happily, waving her hands for no reason whatsoever. Whitney smiled. Count your blessings, she told herself. You're looking at the biggest one right now.

The youth center had been transformed from the brightly wrapped Christmas present it had been only a few days before. Now it looked like a gaudy disco palace. Whitney smiled to herself as she walked through the large hall. Obviously, the kids equated New Year's with glitter.

"Whitney!"

A high-pitched voice shrieked out her name from across the room, and Whitney immediately saw Zoë running toward her. As she was enveloped in a bear hug, Whitney couldn't help but think how different Zoë seemed from the first time they met. She was still wearing mostly black, but a bright red T-shirt under her leather jacket brought out the color in her cheeks. More importantly, though, Zoë's eyes had come to life. The girl had always been talkative and animated, but now her enthusiasm didn't seem so worked up. Now the excitement seemed real.

"Happy new year!" Whitney said. "Where are the guys?"

"Oh, they're around here somewhere," Zoë dismissed them with a wave of her hand. "I'm sure we'll see them soon. But there's someone else here I want you to meet."

Zoë looked around, and Whitney got herself ready. As well as Zoë seemed to be doing, Whitney fervently hoped she wasn't going to introduce her to a boyfriend. She was still so young, and emotionally Whitney didn't think she was anywhere near ready for a romantic relationship.

"There she is. Mom!" Zoë called across the room, waving her arms wildly.

Whitney managed to hide her surprise as she watched Zoë's mother walk toward them. The facial resemblance between the two was remarkable. They had the same strong jaw line, slim nose, and thick eyebrows over gray-blue eyes. But there the resemblance stopped. The woman walked toward them calmly, almost primly, and was dressed in a conservative winter pants suit. Whitney half expected her to be cold, but as soon as she reached Zoë, she slipped her arm around her daughter's shoulders and gave her a squeeze.

"What's up, hon?" she asked with a smile.

"Mom, I wanted you to meet my friend, Whitney."

The woman's eyes grew wide and her smile broader as she

held her hand out to Whitney. "Well, at long last we meet. I'm Gwen."

Whitney took her hand. "It's great to meet you, Gwen. And this is Katie," she said with a nod to the baby, who was sleeping in her buggy.

"Isn't she a doll?" Zoë asked. Then she noticed someone across the room. "Hey, I see Ron. I'll be right back." And she was off, dashing across the hall.

Whitney laughed. "She certainly has a lot of energy."

Gwen nodded, her face suddenly somber. "Yes, she does. But she's only just getting to be like her old self." She stopped, as though unsure what to say, then continued on. "You're a big part of that. Thank you."

Whitney wasn't quite sure how to respond. "I don't know that I did all that much. Actually, your daughter and her friends helped me out."

"Yes, but the point is that you let them." Gwen gave a sad smile. "Most people take a look at kids like her and just assume they're bad. They don't stop to think maybe there's a reason for the crazy outfits and the attitude. But you didn't assume anything. That took a lot of guts."

"You know what I think?" Whitney said softly. "I just think God put us all together that night because he knew we could help each other."

Gwen held up her hands as if not quite sure that she wanted to admit God would do something good in her life. "Whatever the reason, it turned Zoë around. We've still got our issues, but at least now she's talking to me. You gave me my daughter back."

Whitney was feeling overwhelmed by the woman's words, so it was with great relief that she saw Zoë and Ron jogging up to her.

The four talked for a little while. She asked about Otis and Jake. Gwen told her about a Web site for new moms that had lots of advice and tips on it. And finally Zoë asked the question Whitney had hoped wouldn't come up.

"How's your friend Doug?"

Whitney felt her face flush hot, but she managed to keep a controlled smile on her face. "Good, I think. Actually, I haven't seen him lately."

Zoë was about ready to ask another question, but Ron seemed to understand that Whitney was feeling uncomfortable, so he cut in.

"He's probably just trying to find you something that will top the bear."

"Bear?" Whitney questioned. "What bear?"

"That huge stuffed teddy bear he got for you at the hospital," Zoë answered.

Whitney thought back to the day Katie was born. The teens had left her room before she'd gotten the bear. "How did you know about that?"

"After we left your room, we ran into him in the hall," Zoë said.

"Literally," Ron said with a snort. "He had his hands so full of things, he could hardly see where he was going."

"Yeah," Zoë agreed. "And he sure was hot to get to your room. But we warned him you were feeding the baby." Her voice dropped at the mere thought of it. "I hope he didn't walk in on you doing that."

Whitney shook her head. "No, he didn't." This didn't make sense. Obviously, Doug had intended to see her. According to the kids, he was even excited about it. So what changed everything so drastically?

She wanted to think through this new information, but the director of the youth center approached them and she had to pay attention to him. A jovial, heavyset man, he had heard all about Whitney from her young friends.

"To hear them tell it," he said, "you almost had that baby right in the mall."

Whitney smiled. "It wasn't quite that close, but I can't tell you how much they helped me. Just being able to sit with them and chat kept me from concentrating on anything negative."

They talked a little longer, and by the time the man excused himself to converse with someone else, Whitney had promised to call the activities director in the next week about setting up some art and photography classes. She spent the rest of the evening mingling and making small talk until she felt she could politely say her good-byes and leave.

As she drove home, her mind went back to Doug. Why hadn't he come to see her in the hospital when that had obviously been his intention? What had happened to change his feelings? Over and over, she replayed the day in her mind, but the memories were still twisted in knots that she couldn't untangle.

Once inside the house, Whitney laid Katie in her bassinet. She knew she should go to sleep too, but her mind was too restless. So she put on her painting clothes and went into her studio. There in the corner was the picture she'd been working on the first week that Doug had been home. Try as she might, she still hadn't been able to figure out how to finish it.

Now, as she stared at the painting, Whitney replayed the events of the last few months over in her head. As though she were watching a movie, images of Doug flashed by until finally she got to Katie's birthday. She went through every piece of it and, slowly, it all fell into place.

And just about the same time she figured out what had happened to scare Doug off, she finally realized what was missing from the picture in front of her.

CHAPTER 19

It was New Year's Eve, and Doug was going in circles.

He sat astride a chocolate brown Arabian stallion that was having a grand time frisking in his first Montana winter. Doug held on tightly with his thighs as the horse turned round and round, snorting and pawing at the snow.

"Did I buy myself a work horse or a carousel pony?" He spoke to the animal in soft, even tones and patted his neck firmly. The name on the horse's registration was Desert Sun, but Doug had decided to call him Sunny. Not that it matched his disposition, at least not initially. When Doug had first seen him in Kalispell, he wasn't looking for another horse. He had already arranged to purchase several mares, but on his way to the business office he had to go through the stable. That's when he'd noticed the stallion biting the heck out of his stall door.

"Just got him in from California," the stable manager had told him. "They must not have treated him very well, cuz he doesn't much like people."

Right then, Doug had decided this was the horse for him. He needed a project to pour himself into, and Sunny needed someone who would give him a lot of attention.

All and all, his trip to find new stock had been successful, even if it had made him miss Christmas with the family. But that was just as well. Whitney had been there, and he really didn't want to face her yet. Sure, he knew they'd have to see each other eventually. But he hoped that, given enough time, the pain would lessen. Maybe he'd even forget.

Doug laughed bitterly, causing Sunny to jerk his head up. "Sure, as if you can ever forget the love of your life."

Sunny shook his head, and Doug gave him another pat. "See? I knew you and I would make a good team. Okay, boy, that's enough snow for today." He pulled the reins gently to the left and rode toward the barn.

But then he heard the house's screen door slam closed with a bang, and out of the corner of his eye could see someone running toward him, arms waving wildly. He immediately began stroking Sunny's neck, and then called out to the person as calmly as possible.

"If you don't slow down, you're going to spook him."

Now Doug could see it was his mother. She stopped waving her hands, but walked toward them at a fast clip and stopped at the corral rail, breathing heavily.

"What's the big emergency?" Doug asked.

Myra put her hand to her chest, catching her breath. "Whitney. She just called."

His brows furrowed. He hadn't heard from her since that day in the hospital. Even though it had been his idea to break things off, it still hurt him that she hadn't reached out in any way. But now this. Would she always call him whenever she needed something? "What, is she out of milk? Need a ride into town?" He hated himself for the sarcastic edge that hung on his words.

"No," Myra said with a frown. "It's Katie. She said there's something wrong with Katie."

Doug no longer cared if he was being used or not. He loved that little girl like she was his own. He couldn't waste another second. "Open the gate, Mom, and stand back."

As Myra did so, Doug said to Sunny, "Now we're going to see just how well you handle the white stuff."

The next moment they were flying out of the corral and down

the path behind the house toward Whitney's home.

The pounding of Doug's heart matched the beat of the horse's hooves as they hit the ground heavy, hard, and fast. How could he have been so stupid? Doug silently berated himself for his actions. Whether or not he and Whitney had a future together, there was still Katie to consider, and the fact that he'd told Whitney he'd be there whenever she needed him. But his pride had been wounded, so he'd run, just like always. Dear God, he prayed, forgive me for being such a fool. Keep Katie safe. Please don't let me be too late, whatever it is.

Five minutes later he pulled Sunny up short in front of the house. He quickly dismounted and ran to the front door. He jerked on the knob, but it wouldn't budge. Doug swore under his breath. She picked a fine time to start locking her door!

"Whitney!" he yelled. "I'm here. Hold on!" And with that he gathered himself together and hurled himself against the door.

It gave way with a splintering of wood, ripping the latch right out of the framework. Standing at the other end of the room was Whitney. She had a look of utter shock on her face and was holding a contented looking Katie in her arms.

They stared at each other for a moment before Whitney spoke. "I was on my way to get the door."

Doug shook his head. He struggled to get his breathing and his emotions under control. "Katie," he said, pointing. "Mom said . . . but she looks fine. I thought she was sick."

Whitney smiled, "No, she's one-hundred-percent healthy."

Doug felt himself flush red with anger. "What kind of game are you playing? I thought she was dying!"

Whitney frowned. "I'm sorry, Doug. I didn't mean to mislead you, but I didn't know how else to get you over here. I didn't think you'd come if you thought I just wanted to talk to you. So I enlisted your mother's help."

"You lied to me," Doug said in amazement. "You said there

was something wrong with Katie."

"There is something wrong with Katie, but it's not physical." At the confused look on his face, she continued. "Katie needs a father, Doug. That's what's wrong. She needs you."

Doug's heart sank. How long would this charade go on? "Whitney, I know you'd like a father for Katie, but I can't be that man. It would hurt too much, knowing the way you feel."

Whitney smiled softly and put Katie down in the bassinet beside her. Then she walked up to Doug, her arms crossed in front of her. "Oh really? And just how do I feel?"

Why was she making him say it? They both knew, but he supposed it was better to get it out in the open than lie about it. "I know that you still love Cliff. That you'll always love Cliff. Face it, I'd never be more than a stand-in, and I can't live like that."

She took another step toward him and put her hands on his shoulders. "Doug," she said, looking into his eyes, "you've got to promise me that if we're going to make this marriage work, we can't keep secrets from each other."

Now Doug was totally lost. "Excuse me?"

Her eyes twinkled. "Somehow, you've got this crazy notion that I'm only using you as a surrogate for Cliff. I think you overheard me talking to Katie at the hospital. Is that right?"

Doug didn't know what to say, so he just nodded.

"But you didn't hear all of it. What you don't realize is that I was saying good-bye to Cliff. Forever. Because I want nothing more than to start a new life with you."

"Are you totally sure?" Doug's voice was raspy and heavy with hope.

"I love you, Douglas Poulten." With that she pulled his face down to hers and kissed him, sealing her promise of love.

"Marry me?" Doug asked, looking into her eyes. They were filled with love and tears as she nodded her head.

Doug pulled Whitney tight against him. Thank you, Lord, he

prayed. You've turned my life around again.

"Doug," her voice was low and sweet in his ear.

"Hmm?"

"You're going to have to buy me a new door."

He pulled away from her long enough to look at the mess he'd made earlier. With a chuckle, he asked, "How 'bout I just buy you a whole new house? I mean, this is a great place, but it's not really big enough, is it?"

"I don't know," she answered playfully. "How much room will we need?"

He shrugged. "I don't know. Room for at least a few more kids, if that's okay with you."

"Oh, yeah," she said, preparing to kiss him again. "That's definitely okay with me."

Then Doug noticed the picture that hung over her mantle and walked over to look at it. "Hey, you finished it." It was the painting she'd been working on when he'd first come home, only she had added something to it. Now there was a family having a picnic by the creek. The mother was sitting on an old horse blanket, watching as the father stood by the water, showing the little girl how to skip rocks.

A smile crept over his face. "That's us, isn't it?"

She walked up next to him, putting an arm around his back and laying her head on his shoulder. "Yep," she said contentedly. "I finally figured out what was missing from the picture."

EPILOGUE

"And we're finished."

Whitney made one final brush stroke, then stood back to survey the finished product. The Noah mural on the wall of the church nursery was done and, thankfully, Noah was no longer scowling.

Brushing a stray lock of hair from her forehead with the back of her hand, Whitney looked over at the young man standing next to her. The look on Jake's face was indescribable. "So what do you think?" she asked him.

One corner of his mouth turned up in a reluctant grin. "I can't believe we painted all that."

Whitney nodded in agreement. "Amazing, isn't it? And just think, a few months ago, we didn't even know you could paint."

Not for the first time, Whitney silently thanked God for the change he'd brought about in Jake's life. When she'd started giving painting classes at the youth center, Jake had surprised her by signing up. When she'd told him how glad she was that he was there, the reticent young man had just shrugged. It hadn't taken her long, though, to realize the talent that was buried inside him.

At first his paintings and sketches had been dark. Considering the emotional turmoil he'd been through, this came as no surprise. But she did want to do something to draw him out and encourage him to explore more positive emotions. That's when she'd gotten the idea of asking him to help her with the

Noah mural.

Whitney always experienced a surge of satisfaction when she completed a project. Now, seeing the look of pride on Jake's face made that feeling all the more sweet. Once again, she'd received just as much, if not more, out of helping Jake as the teen had.

She put one hand on her hip and made a show out of looking the wall over. "Hmm. There is one thing missing."

Jake turned to her with concern. "What?"

She held out a fine-tipped brush to him. "It needs the signature of the artist."

The smile was back on his face as he took the brush and found a place on the wall to make his mark. As Whitney watched him sign his name near the bottom of the ark, she heard a familiar sound in the hall.

"Who could that be?" she said in mock innocence, turning around.

Doug appeared in the doorway, holding Katie against his hip. "It's your family," he said with a grin. "We wanted to see how you two were doing."

"See for yourself." She made a grand gesture with one hand toward the painted wall.

"Wow." Doug put Katie in the nearby baby swing and walked up to Whitney's side. Slipping his arm around her, he squeezed her tightly. "You did an incredible job. Both of you. Great job, Jake."

The youth turned toward them, obviously proud that Doug had acknowledged him. "Thanks, Mr. Poulten." Jake looked at his watch and asked Whitney, "If we're done, can I go now?"

"Sure," she said with a nod. "Do you need a ride home?"

"No." He hesitated for a moment before continuing. "I've got an appointment with Pastor Rogers. After that, my dad's going to pick me up and we're going to Bernie's."

Whitney was thrilled. Not only was Jake going to talk to Pastor, he was also going to spend some one-on-one time with his father. But she didn't want to make a big deal out of it and spook him. "Okay," she replied simply. "Then I'll see you next week for art class."

"Yep. Bye." With typical teenage energy, he was out the door and halfway down the steps before Doug and Whitney could say their good-byes in return.

The couple stood for a moment, their arms around each other, gazing at the painting. Whitney looked at the rainbow and couldn't help but think what a perfect symbol that was for her. She'd gone through the storm of her life, and God had brought her through and blessed her more than she had ever dreamed.

Things had fallen into place so quickly for her and Doug after they talked things through. As soon as Doug fixed her door well enough to close it, they'd gone to his parents' house to ring in the New Year. On the stroke of midnight, they'd announced their engagement, immediately sending the entire family into a flurry of excitement.

The next Sunday at church, they'd found out the property bordering the Poulten ranch was for sale. Since the Hinkleys were old friends of the family, it hadn't taken long to pound out the details and arrange for that to be Doug and Whitney's new home. Three months later, in early March, the couple was married in a small family service.

Now here Whitney stood, with her husband beside her, her daughter cooing happily in the swing behind them, and more good news to share. It was suddenly too much to contain.

Whitney turned so that she was in front of Doug and threw both arms around him. "Have I told you today that I love you, Douglas Poulten?"

His eyes flashed and a smile took over his face. "Let me

think. . . . Yes, I think you did this morning. Several times in fact."

"Really?" she purred back. "Then let me tell you again."

She pulled his head down to hers and kissed him. For a rugged man, he had the softest lips imaginable, and as always, Whitney lost herself in him. When they finally broke from the kiss, they were both breathing a little harder than usual.

Doug circled her waist with his hands. "I do like being able to hold you close. You were beautiful when you were pregnant, but it sure was hard to hug you."

"This is nice," she said playfully, "but don't get used to it."

Doug froze and pushed her gently away from him. "Are you saying what I think you're saying?"

She was enjoying this. "That depends. What do you think I'm saying?"

A low growl of frustration rumbled deep in Doug's throat. "Woman, you are so exasperating sometimes."

"Okay, okay," she said with a laugh. "I won't torture you anymore. I'm pregnant." She became serious and put her hand on his cheek. "We're going to have a baby."

"Ah, Whit." He hugged her tightly, then gave a whoop of joy, picked her up off her feet and twirled her around.

Whitney was laughing when he set her down, but Doug had become deadly serious. "I'm sorry, I probably shouldn't have done that." He put his hand gently on her still-flat stomach. "Do you think I hurt the baby?"

Whitney rolled her eyes. "Of course not, Doug. I'm not made of glass."

"I know, but we still need to be careful." He put his hand on her elbow and turned her toward the door. When she stooped to get Katie out of the swing, Doug stopped her. "You're not supposed to do any heavy lifting."

Whitney almost argued with him, but thought better of it.

She knew him well enough to expect more of this in the months ahead. It would be seven months of her husband waiting on her hand and foot, answering to her every whim. Which, come to think about it, might not be bad at all.

ABOUT THE AUTHOR

Jennifer AlLee lives in Las Vegas, Nevada, with her husband and teenage son. When she's not writing, Jennifer enjoys spending time with her family, reading, and catching an occasional movie.